Simple Assault
& Buttery

Jan Fields

Annie's®
AnniesFiction.com

Books in the Chocolate Shoppe Mysteries series

Library of Congress-in-Publication Data
Simple Assault & Buttery / by Jan Fields
p. cm.
I. Title
2017957374

AnniesFiction.com
(800) 282-6643
Chocolate Shoppe Mysteries™
Series Creator: Shari Lohner
Series Editors: Janice Tate, Ken Tate
Cover Illustrator: Bonnie Leick

10 11 12 13 14 | Printed in South Korea | 9 8 7 6 5 4

Morning sunshine poured through the front windows of The Chocolate Shoppe Bakery and spilled over the mostly filled tables and chairs scattered around the customer area. The bakery was busy, which was nothing unusual. Moss Hollow's residents claimed it had the best breads and pastries in Nathan County, thanks to a combination of old family recipes and frequent additions of new treats to keep the selection interesting.

Behind the front counter, Jillian Green pasted a smile on her face as she listened to Mellie Flanigan complain about the éclairs she'd bought at Sweeties, a bakery in Painter's Ridge. Jillian wasn't sure what the correct response was to complaints about someone else's product. She didn't want to talk down another business, but she had no idea why someone would drive all the way to Painter's Ridge for baked goods, and she tended to think Mellie deserved what she got for doing it.

"The filling was uneven too," Mellie said, leaning over the counter for emphasis. "Half of them barely had anything inside at all."

"That must have been disappointing," Jillian said, grasping at an opportunity to stem the flow of complaints. "Would you like some of our éclairs today? I can assure you they are all perfectly filled."

Mellie frowned at the display case. "I don't know. Those éclairs from Sweeties really put me off. It may be awhile before I'm ready for éclairs again. You know, I'm not even sure the chocolate drizzle on top was real chocolate."

"Do you know what you *would* like today?" Jillian asked. She could hear the faint tension in her own voice. She hoped Mellie would miss it, but from the sharp glance she received, Jillian suspected the other woman had caught the edge in her voice.

"Are the doughnuts fresh?" Mellie asked, eyeing the goods suspiciously.

Jillian's smile was beginning to hurt the corners of her mouth. "Yes, ma'am. We bake them fresh every morning. Since they sell out early, there's not much chance we'd be able to carry them over even if we wanted to."

"Good," Mellie said. "I believe those éclairs I got from Sweeties were a day old. They were in the main case, and the counter girl told me they were fresh, but I could tell the difference. They were hard and crumbly."

Jillian dropped her hands to the counter in front of her and asked, "Just out of curiosity, why did you go to Sweeties?"

"Well, I was in Painter's Ridge at the podiatrist, and his office was right next to Sweeties." She shrugged. "It was an impulse buy."

"Understandable. We've all made choices we regret." *Like agreeing to work the front counter this morning.* Jillian smiled, making a determined effort to force cheer into her voice. "So, can I get you some doughnuts today?"

Again Mellie peered into the display case. Jillian saw the two customers in line behind Mellie were beginning to get annoyed. "Just pick something already," Gordon Sprague insisted. Gordon was a retired math teacher from Moss Hollow High School, and he had already shown more patience than Jillian had ever seen from him in high school. "You'd think you were picking out your casket. It's just pastry, Mellie! Pick something and get going!"

Mellie gave him a dirty look. "You wouldn't say that if you'd been through what I went through with those horrible éclairs from Sweeties. Pastry matters."

Jillian wanted to drop her head into her arms as the customers began arguing about the relative importance of good pastries. *Why did Maggie pick now to get the flu?*

Jillian didn't belong in the front of the bakery. Maggie was so good at wrangling people like Mellie, but it wasn't Jillian's strong suit. For a long time, she had suspected she wasn't going to be good at anything related to the bakery, but she'd finally connected with her inner baker and could now produce most of the bakery's line without mishap. Still, with Maggie out for the day and with Jillian being the slowest baker in the kitchen, it made sense for her to work the front counter. At least, it had made sense before she actually slipped off the hairnet and pasted on the smile.

A sharp clap from behind her made Jillian jump and spin to face her grandmother. Bertie Harper spread her fiercest glare among the loud customers. "Is there some reason y'all are squabbling in my bakery?"

"I do apologize, Miss Bertie," Mellie said, her tone suddenly sweet and humble. "I was just trying to purchase some baked goods, and Mr. Sprague felt it was appropriate to scold me like I was one of his students."

"You *were* one of my students," Gordon replied, "and not that long ago, young lady."

Considering Mellie had to be pushing fifty, Jillian thought Gordon had an interesting definition of "not that long ago." Of course, Gordon Sprague had seemed ancient to Jillian when she was in high school, so she supposed time was relative.

Bertie walked to the counter and clapped her hands again to bring the attention back to herself. "What do you want to buy today, Mellie?"

"Not éclairs!" Mellie said.

Bertie's frown deepened. "If you're going to order by listing all the things you are *not* going to buy, I can see why Gordon is getting annoyed. What do you want?"

Mellie sniffed. "Muffins. Two blueberry and two chocolate chip."

"Excellent." Bertie patted Jillian's shoulder. "Jillian will get that right away."

For a moment, Jillian gaped at her grandmother. *Why did I expend so much energy in trying to be nice? Apparently bossy is the way to go.*

"Yes ma'am." Jillian hurried to stuff the muffins in a bag before Bertie could go back to the kitchen. Mellie might change her mind once her grandmother's sour countenance was no longer in sight. As she handed over the muffins, Mellie responded to Jillian's "thank you" with a harrumph.

"Are we all good now?" Bertie asked.

"Yes, ma'am," Jillian said. It was the best thing to say to Bertie in her current mood. "Do you know if Celia will be here soon?" The teenager helped out at the bakery in the afternoons. Once she arrived, Jillian could hide out in the kitchen.

Bertie narrowed her eyes. "Celia will get here when school's out. It's not even lunchtime yet. Buck up." She bustled off to the kitchen, and Jillian gazed after her bleakly.

"Miss Green?" Gordon said. "Do you suppose I could get some of those doughnuts?"

Jillian pasted the smile back on her face. "Of course. How many can I get you?"

The stream of customers through the bakery was a testimony to the weather. One of the problems with working the front counter was that Jillian could see the beautiful day outside. Sure, it was already December, but in Moss Hollow, Georgia, that merely meant the nights were cold enough for a coat and the days were prone to rain. But on clear days, the sunshine could tempt even the most antisocial curmudgeon outside, and the streets were bustling with Christmas shoppers. As she forced smiles and slipped baked goods into bags and boxes, Jillian felt the pull of the beautiful weather as much as anyone.

Finally she had a moment of breathing room when no one stood at the counter waiting for a sweet-tooth cure. Jillian poured herself a cup of coffee to celebrate and sipped it as she gazed over the customers seated at the tables. Even Stewie Franks kept pausing in his careful read of the Atlanta newspaper to stare out the window at the morning sunshine. Usually nothing could distract Stewie from his newspaper. In fact, he took out his hearing aids every day during his reading so the chatter of the customers wouldn't interrupt his enjoyment of the day's media mayhem.

Gordon and Stewie were the only people who had tables to themselves. The rest were taken up with pairs of women with shopping bags leaning against their chairs. Jillian wondered idly when she'd have some time for a little Christmas shopping. She still needed to pick out something for Hunter. She had no idea what to get him. Men were so tough to buy for.

The bakery door swung open, making the little bell jingle, and Bonnie Steck hurried in. The owner of Splish Splash, the local coin laundry, Bonnie tended to be almost as no-nonsense as Bertie, and even grumpier. She headed toward the counter with her usual rocking gait caused by sore hip joints. She slapped a piece of paper down on the counter. "Have y'all gotten one of these yet?"

Jillian expected a recipe or perhaps a photo cut from a cooking magazine. Instead, the paper was a short note, written in careful block letters. She read it aloud, "'No, no, no; their offers should not charm us. Their evil gifts would harm us.'" She looked back up at Bonnie, puzzled. "You having a poetry contest down at the coin laundry?"

"Hardly," Bonnie said. "Someone shoved this under my door this morning. Check out the other side."

The back side of the note had five words: *One had a cat's face.*

Jillian shrugged. "If this is supposed to be a message about your laundry, it's not exactly clear."

"I don't know what it's supposed to be about," Bonnie said. "But it's creepy. I was so discombobulated, I could barely make change for my first customer." She turned to Gordon Sprague, who sat at a table nearby. "Isn't that right?"

The retired teacher rolled his eyes in an amazing impression of the teenagers he used to teach. "I didn't see any difference in your usual math skills."

"Oh hush up, you old coot," Bonnie grumbled.

"You invited me into the conversation," Gordon shot back.

Bonnie ignored him and said to Jillian, "I'm not the only one who has gotten a note like that."

Jillian raised her eyebrows. "This is the first I've heard about it. Do they all say the same thing? A rhyme about gifts and offers and a sentence about a cat?"

Bonnie shook her head. "They all rhyme, or at least one side does. And they all have different animals. Lisa Flint from Print Worthy got something about the voice of doves, but I haven't seen any of the others. I think we need to talk to the town council about this. Something needs to be done."

"About rhyming notes?" Jillian asked.

"They're creepy. Anonymous notes are creepy, and the verse is creepy, and I don't much like being described as having a cat's face."

Jillian thought the comparison of Bonnie's round face and pug nose to a cat wasn't completely unfair, but she kept that opinion to herself.

"It's probably someone with time on his hands and a weird fondness for rhymes," Jillian said. "There's nothing particularly threatening about it."

"That's what Deputy Jones said." The annoyance in Bonnie's tone grew stronger. "He didn't take it seriously at all. He told me the sheriff's department didn't handle love notes or greeting cards either." She folded her arms over her ample chest. "Don't think I didn't write a strongly worded note to Sheriff Henderson about the deputy's attitude."

Jillian almost asked her if her note to the sheriff rhymed, but she doubted Bonnie would find that amusing. So she tried for a more concerned expression, or at least she hoped that was what she was reflecting. "I do think it probably isn't really a matter for the sheriff's department. Have you seen anyone hanging around?"

Bonnie rolled her eyes. "I run a coin laundry. People are always hanging around."

"Anyone acting shifty?" Jillian clarified.

"Again, coin laundry. Half my regular clientele acts a bit shifty." She snatched the note from the counter and wagged her finger at Jillian. "I can tell you're not taking this seriously either. Mark my words, you'll feel differently when one of these shows up at the bakery."

"One already has."

Jillian spun to gape at her grandmother. "Really? Why didn't I hear about it?"

"Because it's silly," Bertie said. "And it's not like no one in our family has ever gotten an anonymous note before. This one didn't threaten bodily harm, wasn't scrawled on the floor in blood, and even rhymed."

Jillian had to admit, she had gotten more than her share of anonymous threats since moving home from California, though none of them had actually been written in blood and she wasn't sure her grandmother should be giving anyone any ideas. Jillian kept finding herself in the middle of problems through no fault of her own, and too many of those came with threats. Still, a rhyming note was new. "What did ours say?"

Bertie sighed and walked over to a small side counter. She pulled open a drawer, retrieved a folded piece of paper, and thrust it at Jillian. "It's not exactly enlightening."

Jillian saw the block lettering was identical to Bonnie's note. So was the paper. She read the note aloud, "'Come buy, come buy; taste them and try. Sweet to tongue and sound to eye; come buy, come buy.'" She shrugged. "Sounds like a bakery to me."

Bonnie leaned closer, squinting at the paper. "Anything about an animal?"

Jillian flipped over the note. "'One like a ratel tumbled hurry-skurry.' What's a ratel?"

"I looked it up on my smartphone," Bertie said, and Jillian could tell she was rather proud of thinking to do that. "It's another name for the honey badger."

"Which of us do you figure the writer is calling a honey badger?"

Bertie shrugged.

"So, what are you going to do about the note?" Bonnie asked.

"I'm going to stick it back in the drawer," Bertie answered. "It's not worth our attention. Honestly, Bonnie, it's just some strange poetry written by someone with too much time on their hands."

A young woman at a nearby table cleared her throat. "Actually, those are lines from 'Goblin Market.'"

Everyone stared at her in surprise. The woman's cheeks pinked slightly. "I was an English major in college. I know the poem. It's by Christina Rossetti."

"And the stuff about the cat face and the honey badger?" Jillian asked.

"Those are bits from the poem too," the woman said. "I don't have the whole poem memorized. It's really long, but those lines sounded familiar, and I remembered having to look up 'ratel' back when I first read it."

"That doesn't make this any less weird," Bonnie said. "I'm going to call the sheriff's department and let them know. There could be a clue to all this in the rest of the poem."

"I'm sure Gooder will be thrilled," Jillian said. Bonnie gave her a pinched frown, so Jillian tried for a pleasant smile. "Did you want anything else?"

For a moment, she thought Bonnie might refuse and storm out, but finally the shorter woman deflated a bit and said, "Give me a couple of those pumpkin cookies and a cup of coffee to go."

While Jillian gathered Bonnie's order, Bertie shoved the note into the drawer and spent a minute checking all the display cases to see what might need restocking. After Bonnie carried out her little white bag of cookies and cup of coffee, Jillian whispered to Bertie. "The whole note thing is a little weird."

Bertie flapped a hand at her. "It's nothing."

"Really? Then why did you keep it?"

Bertie harrumphed. "Because I'm old enough to know that even if something starts out as nothing, we never know where it could end up. I believe in being prepared."

"Sounds reasonable," Jillian said, but how it really sounded was ominous. Surely her grandmother wasn't really worried about some note that quoted a poem? And surely Jillian shouldn't be worried about it as well.

Too late, she thought gloomily. *I'm already worrying.*

After a long week of wishing Maggie would hurry up and get well, Jillian was seriously ready for a nice quiet evening at home with a book and maybe Belle Haven's resident cat, Possum, in her lap. Instead, she stood in the kitchen of Belle Haven, her coffee mug clutched in her hand and her mouth hanging open. "You want to go where?"

Bertie barely gave her a glance as she poured her own cup of coffee. "Stop being so dramatic. We're going to the town council meeting. We probably should go to more of them. We are business owners in Moss Hollow after all."

"By more of them you mean more than none?" Jillian asked. "Because I remember you clearly saying that town council meetings were like nonaddictive sleeping pills."

"Well, I agree with Bertie this time."

Jillian stared at her great-aunt. First, it was rare that Cornelia Montgomery agreed with her twin sister on *anything*. And second, Cornelia was the least tolerant person Jillian knew when it came to being bored. "You want to go to the town council meeting too?"

"I think we all should." Cornelia sat perched on one of the kitchen stools, peering at them over the rim of her teacup. "I've been concerned about those weird notes. I've consulted the tear-out cards and the results are ominous."

Jillian groaned. "The only ominous thing about those subscription cards you tore out of magazines is that you think they can pass along messages from the spirit realm."

Cornelia sniffed. "You don't have to be so dismissive. You know, you used to have a more open mind."

"Really?" Jillian said. "When?"

"Maybe I'm confusing you with your mother," Cornelia said.

Now you're just being insulting. Jillian's relationship with her mother varied from tense to nonexistent. Especially since she and Jillian's dad had sold their house years ago when Jillian was fresh out of high school to take up a nomadic existence, crisscrossing the country in search of "new experiences."

Bertie stirred sugar into her coffee, the spoon ringing against the sides of the mug. "We've wandered off topic. You know a number of the other business owners are worried about the notes. Some of them are quite vocal about it, and I'm growing concerned about the mood of the town. We're going as a show of support, and because they may benefit from a voice of reason."

"That's not why I'm going," Cornelia said.

"That's all right, Cornelia," Bertie told her. "No one expects you to be the voice of reason."

"How many businesses have gotten the notes?" Jillian asked before Cornelia could take Bertie's bait. "Do you know?"

"All of them," Bertie answered. "Or at least everyone I've spoken with. Jillian, has Hunter gotten one? No one seems to know."

Hunter Greyson was both a mortician and the county coroner. He was also Jillian's boyfriend, though she winced every time she used the word. *Forty-year-old women shouldn't have "boyfriends."* Society really needed to come up with a new name for dating in your forties that sounded neither risqué nor high-schoolish.

Of course, part of her unease about dating Hunter was directly tied to his work. She'd never imagined she'd be in a relationship with a man who spent his workdays around dead people. Not that it wasn't a respected profession. Greyson & Sons Funeral Home was a long-established business in Moss Hollow, and Hunter had relocated from Atlanta to run it for his family. Though he was well-liked in Moss Hollow, people still tended to like him from a distance. *Occupational hazard.* Jillian wasn't sure if that was just the normal disquiet with morticians, or if it stemmed from the somewhat clannish nature of small towns.

"Hunter would certainly not be interested in gossiping about crazy notes," Jillian said.

"But has he gotten one?"

Jillian sighed. "He got one. It was a cheery bit about daisies planted on a grave that never blow."

"Have you read the whole poem?" Cornelia asked as she set her teacup on the counter. "I found it online. It's a story of two sisters. One sister is bewitched by the fairies and goblins and the other sister saves her. It has a happy ending."

"Why would anyone send businesses bits of a fairy-tale poem?" Bertie asked. "It makes no sense. I assume it's some prank, but it certainly is an odd choice."

Jillian drained the last of the coffee from her mug. "Well, if we're going to the council meeting, I want to change my clothes and run a brush through my hair. I wouldn't expect Hunter to be there though. He thinks the uproar over the notes is ridiculous, and I agree with him."

The meeting room for the Moss Hollow Town Council looked exactly as Jillian would have expected. Poorly lit by old fluorescent lights, one of which flickered and buzzed in a way that would grate on the nerves within minutes, the room was long and narrow. The horseshoe-shaped desk where the council sat was the fanciest thing she saw, though the slightly faded flags on poles in the corners came a close second. The walls were institutional beige to match the carpet, and rows of folding chairs for the audience added a pop of color, if blue-gray was considered a color.

The mayor sat in the exact center of the arch of the desk, with three council members on each side of him. Every one of them wore a blazer, women included. Jillian didn't know any of the council members particularly well, though they all seemed familiar so she assumed they were bakery regulars. Certainly Gordon Sprague was, though Jillian hadn't known he was on the town council. She supposed he must have gotten bored after retiring from teaching.

Mayor Carl Blackwater eyed the room nervously as it steadily filled up. Jillian doubted the council and the mayor were used to so many people attending the meetings.

None of the audience seemed in any great hurry to sit in the uncomfortable folding chairs, instead standing in clumps and chatting. Jillian recognized most of the group as they were business owners around Moss Hollow. Bonnie was every bit as worked up as she had been at the bakery as she waved her hands around, ranting at Gladys Glenshaw, the owner of Yarn Charm. Gladys kept edging back away from the waving arms, but Bonnie just stepped closer. It looked like they were doing some kind of aggressive folk dance.

Jillian was surprised by one of the familiar faces. Lenora Ryan, who'd worked in The Chocolate Shoppe Bakery for as long as Jillian could remember, stood next to her cousin Jasmine Jackson, the owner of the Clip & Curl Salon. In fact, Lenora seemed to be cousin to a good third of the population of Moss Hollow, including Celia, the teenager who helped out at the bakery. But there was certainly very little family resemblance in Lenora and Jasmine's appearances. Lenora was a tall woman with short salt-and-pepper hair and a round face that reflected her kind heart. Jasmine was tiny next to her cousin and thin as a stick with bright eyes that didn't miss much, despite the cat-eye glasses studded with rhinestones that she wore. Even Jasmine's skin tone was different, more mahogany to Lenora's cherrywood.

Jillian walked over to the pair. "I didn't know you were going to be here."

"I wasn't going to miss it," Jasmine said. "I got that creepy little poem on Wednesday. And when I find out who called me rat-faced, I'm going to thump 'em on the head."

"I believe that's just another quote from the poem," Lenora said gently.

"Well, it felt personal!" Jasmine peered at Jillian through her glasses. "Lenora said the bakery got a note too. What did the note call you?"

"It's a quote from a poem," Jillian said. "I'm not sure it's meant to be name-calling."

Jasmine crossed her arms over her chest. "What did it call you?"

"I don't think it was talking about me," Jillian said. "I don't own the bakery, Bertie does."

"Fine, what did it call Bertie?"

Jillian gave in. "A honey badger."

"A honey badger?" Jasmine squeaked. "Honey badgers are cool! Why didn't they call me a honey badger?"

Lenora patted her cousin's shoulder. "Whoever wrote the note doesn't know you."

"I'd say." Jasmine harrumphed. "Rat-faced. Someone is getting a thump, I tell you."

Jillian's gaze drifted toward the door to the council room, and she got her second surprise of the evening. Hunter walked through the door with Savannah Cantrell. Savannah was Jillian's oldest friend in Moss Hollow. She spotted Jillian and waved. Hunter turned his attention in her direction, and the smile that lit his face brought warmth to Jillian's cheeks.

"What you blushing over?" Jasmine demanded. She followed Jillian's gaze. "Oh, I see. That is one attractive man. I hope you're planning to take him off the market soon."

"You'd best be careful, teasing like that," Lenora warned her cousin. "Jillian might end up thumping *your* head."

"Who said I was teasing?" Jasmine asked. "I was giving genuinely good advice."

Jillian didn't reply to either remark. She simply asked them to excuse her and wove through the crowd to reach Hunter. "This has been an evening of surprises. I didn't think you took those notes seriously."

"I don't," Hunter said. "But I thought it was wise to come out in support of the other business owners."

"You sound like Bertie." Jillian sent a smile at Savannah. "Don't tell me you got a note."

Savannah nodded. "This morning actually. Someone tucked it under my windshield wiper while I was in the grocery. I thought I might miss out since I don't have a storefront, but I guess the poetry fan is determined to include us all."

"Jasmine is up in arms," Jillian said. "Apparently her quote implied she's rat-faced."

Savannah winced. "Mine said I'm parrot-voiced and jolly. I was a little down about that, but I think I prefer it over rat-faced."

"I wouldn't take any of it to heart," Hunter said. "Someone has a very odd sense of humor and is probably delighted to be causing a bit of trouble."

A tapping sound drew their attention to the front of the room. Mayor Blackwater held a gavel, which he used to gesture at the crowd. "Could everyone find a seat, please? We need to begin."

"I'll say we do!" Bonnie shouted.

"Yeah!" Jasmine chimed in.

"Don't worry—we'll have time for everyone to speak their piece. Please." He waved toward the chairs and the crowd moved toward them, though not without some grumbling.

"I'm concerned about how upset people are getting," Hunter said as they walked to the nearest chairs. "If they do figure out who is sending these notes, I don't know what they expect to happen to the person. As far as I know, there is no law against sending people poetry quotations."

"Well, if I find out who sent the miserable thing," Cal Haskell said, clearly overhearing Hunter as he passed by, "I'm going to pop the guy in the nose. I'm not snail-paced, no matter what that note said. I'm just careful in my work." Cal owned the auto shop where Jillian and her family went whenever they had car trouble.

"You shouldn't worry about it," Jillian said. "Everyone knows you have the best auto shop in Nathan County. Bertie says so, and she's not prone to lavish praise."

"Why did the note bother you, Cal?" Hunter asked. "No one would even know what it said if you hadn't told them. All the notes seem to be slipped under doors and into mail slots when no one is around."

Cal shoved his hands into the pockets of his jeans. "Yeah, I know. And it's not like no one has ever complained about something I've done. I think it's the weirdness. It makes it worse." He narrowed his eyes. "What did your note call you?"

"There was no animal reference," Hunter said. "Just the line, 'their looks were evil.'"

"Huh. At least mine didn't say I was evil." He raised an eyebrow at Hunter. "Wonder why yours did."

"Maybe the person simply ran out of animal references," Jillian said. "It's a poem about goblins, not Noah's ark."

"Yeah," Cal said. "You're probably right." But he gave Hunter one more glance before heading toward a chair a row ahead of them.

Great, Jillian thought, *just what this town needed—more paranoia.*

A fresh tapping of the gavel sent the last of the crowd into seats. Jillian was glad she and Hunter were near the back. Savannah had slipped by them and taken a seat next to Lisa Flint from Print Worthy. Jillian knew Savannah did the accounting for the print shop, as well as many of the other shops in Moss Hollow.

The audience muttered and fidgeted through the boring bits of the council meeting, and the council members kept casting nervous glances at the crowd. Finally the mayor gave in and asked if anyone had any new business to bring up. Hands shot up all over the room and Bonnie Steck shot to her feet. "What are you going to do about the notes?"

Mayor Blackwater cleared his throat. "I have been informed about the notes. My office has received copies of several of them. I am a little confused about what you expect us to do about it."

"Find the person doing it!" Bonnie insisted.

"Make them stop!" someone called from the audience.

"Arrest 'em!" someone else shouted. Several people gave loud agreement to that.

"Arrest them for what?" the mayor asked.

"Trespassing!" Bonnie said.

The mayor blinked at her. "Didn't the note come to the laundry?"

"Yes!"

"That's a public business," the major spoke slowly in a measured tone, as if trying to calm a barking dog. "People are allowed to come in during business hours. I don't see how it's trespassing."

"They're allowed to come and do laundry," Bonnie said. "Not leave creepy notes."

"If it's not trespassing," Jasmine called out, "how about harassment?"

"How many notes have you received?" the mayor asked her.

"One," Jasmine admitted. "But we've all gotten one. When you add them up, that's a lot of harassing."

The mayor scanned the room, clearly at a loss for how to calm the angry group. "I've read the notes. There are no threats. Each of you only received one, so it's not a pattern of harassment, and they occur in public places so there's no trespassing. I honestly don't know how we would charge the person, and that's assuming we could determine who is sending them."

"Some nutcase!" Cal yelled.

"Maybe," the mayor said. "But I really think it will all blow over. The person is probably enjoying getting a rise out of everyone."

"He'd enjoy it a lot less if I could figure out who it is," Jasmine said. "I'd smack him."

"Me too!" Bonnie agreed.

"Now, now, there's no need for violence." The mayor smiled at them. "I've asked the sheriff's department to increase patrols for the downtown shops. Beyond that, I really don't think this is an issue for the mayor's office or the town council."

The bulk of the audience clearly disagreed, judging by the booing and grumbling, but they finally settled down and the council meeting dragged to a close. Jillian rubbed her arms, feeling suddenly chilled. She was as curious as anyone about who would send the sometimes insulting quotes to business owners, but she was beginning to hope that they never found out and the notes simply stopped. The mood of the crowd was far more worrying than random bits of verse.

After the meeting, Hunter led Jillian toward the door, but Bonnie stepped in their way, holding up her hands. "What's your hurry? Since it doesn't seem like the mayor is going to do anything, I think we business owners need to take action ourselves."

Hunter frowned down at her. "How do you suggest we do that?"

"You're always poking around and asking nosy questions," Bonnie said. "Why don't you figure out who is sending the notes so we can put a stop to them?"

"I don't know where to begin," Jillian said. "Besides, the mayor has a point. Each shop owner has only gotten one note. It's probably over for you. Why not let it go?"

"Because I don't *know* that it's over," Bonnie snapped. "Maybe this is the first step. Send us all notes, then do something bigger, something worse. What about that?"

"That sounds like worry over something that shows no sign of happening," Hunter said. "Have you considered the possibility that this is some bored teenager trying to stir things up in town?"

"If it is, the kid deserves to be caught and punished. And if you're not going to help, then you're part of the problem as far as I'm concerned." She gave Jillian a shrewd look. "You're usually so quick to want to poke around in things. Is there some reason why you don't want to now? Maybe some personal reason?" She shot a glance at Hunter. "Creepy notes and an undertaker boyfriend might be related."

"Hunter got a note saying he was evil," said Cal, who had been standing nearby. "He'd hardly send something like that to himself."

"Maybe, maybe not." Bonnie appraised Hunter. "He might be trying to deflect attention. Or maybe there's a message in that, and he thinks we're too stupid to get it."

Jillian felt her temper rise at Bonnie's accusations, and she took a step forward, her hands curling into fists at her sides. Hunter stepped between them. "If these notes turn us against one another, then aren't we just playing into the note writer's plan?"

"What plan?" Jillian asked. "If this is some nefarious plan, it's the most obscure one I've ever seen."

"I don't know what the plan might be," Bonnie growled. "But I'll find out. And I'll stop it, no matter who is involved." The angry woman gave Hunter one last glare, then spun on her heel and stomped over to talk to Jasmine.

"I don't like this," Jillian whispered. "I don't like any of this."

By Sunday, Jillian could feel a tension even among the members of the church congregation. There were fewer smiles and more hand wringing. As Jillian walked to her seat, no one reached out to pat her arm or speak to her. Even when she'd first moved back to Moss Hollow and much of the town thought she might have poisoned someone, she had still received a few smiles at church. She couldn't believe anonymous notes containing scraps of poetry could have such an effect. At least back when she was a murder suspect, the town was just suspicious of *her*. Now they seemed to be suspicious of each other.

She settled beside Bertie on the padded pew. "Something has to give soon," she whispered. "The whole town is on edge."

"I've noticed." Bertie twisted around in her seat to look over the congregation. "I hope Pastor Keith will have something to say that helps. People may listen to him when they won't listen to anyone else."

Certainly the pastor tried. He talked about unity and the importance of letting things go, but Jillian saw no more smiles after the service than she did before it, and the few she was offered tended to appear brittle.

Jillian followed Bertie out to the front steps of the church to wait for Cornelia, who had stopped to chat with one of her garden club friends. *At least she's being sociable*, Jillian thought. No one seemed interested in socializing with Jillian or Bertie.

"Once my sister is done gabbing about geraniums, maybe we can go get some lunch," Bertie grumbled. "Then we have to get the bakery ready for the meeting." The Southern Sweetie Pies baking club met at the bakery every Sunday afternoon to talk about baking, to plan events, and frankly, to gossip.

"Do you want to go to the buffet?" Jillian asked. The Southern Peach Inn had a Sunday buffet that was a favorite around town.

"Not today. I'd rather grab something quick. I want to make some notes before the meeting."

"Notes?" Jillian asked.

Bertie nodded. "Maybe the Sweetie Pies can come up with a plan amongst us to help get this town sane again. At the very least, the other business owners need to see that all this suspicion cannot be good for business."

"Bertie Harper!"

Jillian and Bertie turned to see Bonnie storming toward them, followed by several other business owners and even a few other citizens who did not run their own businesses. Jillian spotted Mellie Flanigan in the group, and she knew Mellie didn't own a business. Jillian wasn't even sure she had a job. She wondered how Bonnie had gotten regular people involved. Surely the note writer wasn't expanding the recipient list. The group all wore resolute expressions.

Jillian almost groaned when she spotted Jasmine muscling her way through the crowd to walk side by side with Bonnie. Jasmine and Bonnie were probably the ringleaders, egging each other on. They had the personalities for it.

"What do you want, Bonnie?" Bertie asked, her tone weary.

"We've figured it out!" Bonnie bellowed, stabbing a finger at Bertie. "The poem. It's about you. That's why your granddaughter won't do her duty to the town and ferret out the answer, because she's protecting you!"

Jillian stared in shock at the other woman. She took a step forward, but her grandmother moved faster and planted herself in front of Bonnie.

"What are you talking about?" Bertie demanded.

Bonnie glared at Bertie. "The poem is about two sisters. One sister is under the influence of the fairies, which makes her a little crazy, and the other one takes care of her. Everyone knows you and Cornelia are twins. And everyone knows Cornelia claims to have a connection to *something* otherworldly."

Bertie narrowed her eyes and leaned even closer to Bonnie. The two women were almost exactly matched in height, but no one could match Bertie when it came to sheer force of personality. "You need to leave me and my sister alone. And stop trying to stir up trouble over some silly poem." She waved at the group. "Shame on y'all for acting like this, and in front of the church at that!"

Jillian was pleased to see a few of the people near the back of the group duck their heads and step away. But Bonnie only scowled and gestured toward Cornelia as she walked up with a puzzled expression.

"How do we know it's not *her* sending out the notes?" Bonnie said. "She's loopy enough."

"Hey," Cornelia said. "Simply because I'm open to possibilities does not make me loopy. Perhaps it's you rigid thinkers who are less in touch with true reality."

"Right, like that doesn't sound loopy," Bonnie said.

Jillian was willing to accept that her aunt was a bit eccentric, but she wasn't going to put up with anyone else saying it. And she knew it wouldn't sit well with Bertie either. "There's only one person acting crazy here," Jillian said. "And it's not my aunt."

Bertie drew herself up to her full height and roared, "Enough!" She waved a hand at the group. "Y'all are chasing shadows and picking on your own neighbors over nothing. There's no shortage of sisters in Moss Hollow."

"But no other sisters fit the profile as well as you and Cornelia," Jasmine said, stepping up beside Bonnie with her hands on her hips.

"Really?" Bertie asked. "How about you and Poppy? You two are sisters. And Poppy loves all that fairy stuff."

"That's true," Mellie Flanigan called out. "I drove by Poppy's house last week, and she's got all those fairy silhouettes in her garden. I've never seen so many before."

"That doesn't mean anything. Poppy just thinks they're cute," Jasmine said. "My sister is perfectly normal."

"I dunno," another of the women said. "Didn't she dress up like a fairy for Moss Holloween?"

"And she always seemed a bit off to me," Mellie added. "She's so thin."

"Cause she's sick a lot." Jasmine's voice rose to nearly a shout. "Poppy's always been a little frail."

"That's from the poem too," Mellie insisted. "The sister who is bewitched by the goblins nearly wastes away."

The group was clearly growing more excited by the new theory.

"Stop this now!" Bertie demanded. "You are being ridiculous. Neither Poppy nor Cornelia has anything to do with the notes. You're letting your imaginations run away with you. And over what? Some silly old poetry?"

"Besides, both the bakery and the beauty salon have gotten notes," Jillian said. "Obviously we're all equal in the eyes of whoever is sending the notes. We're all in this together. We're a community, and we shouldn't be attacking one another."

"You would say that if you were trying to deflect attention from your true purpose with those notes," Bonnie said.

"Or maybe she's just on Jasmine's side," Mellie said. "After all, Jasmine's cousin works for the bakery."

"Maybe they're all in on it!" This accusation came from the back of the group, and Jillian couldn't pick out who had said it.

"I've been as upset about the notes as anyone," Jasmine insisted.

"Or you've pretended to be. Joining up with us would surely

be extra helpful in letting *you* avoid suspicion, Jasmine."

"Don't be stupid," Jasmine snapped. "I have nothing to do with those notes."

"Maybe," Bonnie said. She glared back at Bertie. "But I'm thinking they have to do with *some* pair of sisters. And I'm going to figure out which ones. And once I know, I'll put a stop to this business."

"You need to spend less time sniffing laundry detergent, Bonnie Steck," Bertie said, "because there is seriously something wrong with your head."

Bonnie's face reddened, and she was clearly about to blast Bertie when a murmur passed through the group. It divided to allow Pastor Keith to pass through and stand beside Bonnie and Bertie.

"Good morning, ladies." Pastor Keith said with his usual gentle smile. "This seems to be some intense fellowship going on here. Is there a problem I can help you with?"

"No problem, pastor." Bonnie stepped back away from both Bertie and Jasmine. "No problem at all. I was just heading home." She stalked away, her followers trailing her. Jasmine didn't follow the rest of the group. Instead she shot angry glowers in Bertie's direction.

Bertie ignored Jasmine entirely and smiled up at the pastor. "I enjoyed your message this morning. Folks need to remember that we're all one community. Apparently it's easier to forget that than I thought."

The pastor's smile grew. "I am glad to hear you say that. You're a strong force in this community. People follow your lead. That can be a heavy responsibility."

"And it's something you ought to keep in mind, Bertie Harper, before you go throwing out your own theories." Jasmine spun on her heel and marched away.

Jillian was surprised to see Jasmine push by Gordon Sprague, who watched her pass with interest. With an inward groan, Jillian hoped Gordon wasn't about to join in the group of note-crazy citizens.

Pastor Keith watched Jasmine go, his face filled with concern. "Did I say something wrong?"

"These days, I don't know that anyone can say anything right," Bertie told him.

When they gathered in the bakery for their weekly meeting, the Southern Sweetie Pies were buzzing with excitement over the confrontation in front of the church. *They are clearly going to serve up gossip before baking tips today*, Jillian thought.

"That woman had some nerve," Wanda Jean Maplewood huffed. "Maudie and I were talking about it on the way over here."

"How did you two even know about it?" Bertie asked.

Jillian grinned at the question. Maudie Honeycutt and Wanda Jean had been friends for many years, united mostly in their passionate love of gossip, so Jillian wasn't overly surprised they knew about Bonnie's confrontation.

"I ran into Mellie Flanigan at Food for Less," Maudie said. "I stopped to pick up whipped cream for my pie. She was telling anyone who stood still long enough that Jasmine and Poppy were the reason for the creepy notes. She said you said so."

"I certainly did *not* say so," Bertie protested.

"Jasmine called me," Lenora said. "She thinks I should quit my job here at the bakery in family solidarity since Bertie accused her of being the note writer."

Bertie put her hands on her hips, her elbows sticking sharply out to the side like thorns on a particularly irate briar. "That is not what happened *at all*. I was merely trying to show all of them how silly they were acting."

"I didn't say I agreed with Jasmine," Lenora said. "The last time I agreed with Jasmine, we were both in knee-high socks and pigtails. She does have a flair for the dramatic."

"This is getting out of hand," Cornelia said. "The mood at church was troubling, and that crowd outside seemed to be spoiling for a fight. On top of that, my tear-out card readings are becoming increasingly ominous."

Bertie rolled her eyes. "If no one has an idea of how we can work together to quash all this ridiculous business over the notes, I recommend we talk about something else. Gossip is part of the problem. Everyone is talking about these silly notes. If they'd just do the sensible thing and ignore them, we'd be better off."

"We could work on plans for Savannah's wedding," Jillian said, giving her friend a mischievous grin. "It's never too early to get started."

Savannah blushed even as she laughed at Jillian. "Considering James and I haven't set a date yet, I think it's a little early."

"You shouldn't dillydally," Maudie said. "Long engagements are just an invitation for cold feet."

"Well, I don't think she needs to rush," Wanda Jean insisted. Usually Maudie and Wanda Jean were in total agreement on everything, but men were the one area where they diverged. Wanda Jean saw no reason to clutter her life up with a man, and usually held back on the matchmaking that the rest of the Sweetie Pies seemed to enjoy so much. "Far too many women rush into marriage and find themselves saddled with nothing but extra chores."

"I'm not going to rush *or* dillydally," Savannah said calmly. "We're taking it slow so we can have the wedding that is right for us. Now surely there is some more pressing business that we can tackle."

"Yes, there is," said Josi Rosenschein, the local librarian. Josi was always sensitive to teasing and tended to shy away from conflict of any sort. "Let's talk about baking. I would love a good baking project."

Maudie rescued her. "I thought we might talk about the Christmas Bazaar at church. I assume everyone is good with the Sweetie Pies handling the baked goods table again this year?"

The group shifted their attention to the bake sale, some members more reluctantly than others.

"Maybe we should have a theme this year," Annalise Reed suggested. "I always find it more fun to bake and decorate with a theme. Just the other day, I was telling Byron that the bank's holiday decorations would be much more impressive if they chose a theme." Annalise's husband was vice president at the bank.

"Since it's Christmastime, we could borrow a theme from *The Nutcracker*," Josi said quietly. "Maybe something like sugarplum fairies."

"No!" Bertie said quickly, making the librarian jump. "I'm fine with a theme, but after that conversation with Bonnie, I don't want to hear anything about fairies."

"How about an ingredient theme? We could all contribute something with butter," Cornelia suggested. "No one can find butter controversial."

"Really?" Jillian said with a laugh. "When I lived in California, half the people I knew acted like butter was deadly poison."

"Well, we're not in California," Cornelia said with a sniff. "Here in Georgia, everyone is sensible and loves butter. And I make a wonderful chocolate pound cake with tons of butter."

"I could make some chocolate hazelnut croissants," Savannah said. "Or maybe some butter rolls. Not everything in a bake sale has to be sweet."

"Would a yellow cake count?" Maudie asked. "I could do a buttercream frosting. Would that be buttery enough? Or should I just make it a butter cake?"

More butter talk buzzed around the room and Jillian sat back, barely listening. She found she'd caught Cornelia's disquiet over the mood in town. Too many people seemed scared and angry over the notes, which was silly. They were too vague to be threatening, or even particularly insulting. Suddenly Jillian realized who was missing at the meeting. "Laura Lee isn't here."

Jillian didn't even realize she'd spoken aloud until she noticed all eyes on her. "Does Laura Lee have a particularly good recipe for something buttery?" Maudie asked.

"No, sorry, I only just noticed she wasn't here," Jillian said. "Since she's our law enforcement representative, I thought I might chat with her after the meeting."

Bertie raised an eyebrow at her. "If you're thinking you need to talk to her about anything related to the notes, just do it. Maybe the sheriff's department can restore sanity. But for now, we're talking about the church bake sale. Let's stay on task."

Jillian felt her cheeks warm at her grandmother's rebuke. She hadn't actually meant to interject anything about Laura Lee Zane. She'd just been surprised by the young deputy's absence. Of course, Laura Lee had missed club meetings before. Sometimes she had to work, and sometimes she simply had other tasks that took her away from the group. No one came to every single meeting. Still, somehow Jillian felt even more disquieted by Laura Lee's absence than usual that day.

Sirens blared, interrupting the meeting. Several of the Sweetie Pies couldn't resist hurrying to the window to watch the fire trucks and other emergency vehicles pass.

"Maybe it's a brushfire," Lenora said. "Weather's been a bit drier than usual."

"Not dry enough for a brushfire," Maudie argued.

"Maybe if we went outside, we could see the smoke." Cornelia followed up on her suggestion by heading for the door. The rest of the Sweetie Pies followed her out, Bertie throwing up her hands in resignation. They huddled on the street and stared in the direction the trucks had gone. Sure enough, a thin snake of smoke was visible in the near distance.

"Looks like it might be just outside of downtown," Jillian observed.

"There's a florist out that way," Savannah said. "I do their books."

"And Cheap, Cheap Chicken." Lenora fished her cell phone out of her purse. "And the Clip & Curl." She punched buttons and held the phone up to her ear. "Jasmine? What's burning out your way?"

Lenora's eyes widened. "Girl, are you out of your mind? Get out of there! Get out right now!" She ended the call and stared at the Sweetie Pies in horror. "Jasmine says the Clip & Curl is on fire!"

The Sweetie Pies didn't need to be told what to do next. They piled into cars and headed out to the beauty salon. Deputy Tom Shaw stood in the road, trying to direct people away from the scene. He wasn't having much success. The Sweetie Pies didn't ignore him, but they didn't let him send them away either. Instead they parked as close as possible and piled out to cover the rest of the distance on foot.

A crowd already stood gawking while the firemen blasted the outside of the building with water. "Jasmine?" Lenora yelled as she pushed through the crowd. "Anyone seen Jasmine?"

Finally they heard a familiar voice. "Lenora!" Laura Lee yelled. "Your cousin is over here."

Lenora plowed through the crowd. The rest of the Sweetie Pies took advantage of the passage Lenora made and followed her.

The back doors of a local ambulance stood open, and Jasmine was fussing at a young man trying to bandage her hands. "Leave me be! I need to get back inside."

"No one can go inside, ma'am," the emergency tech said. "You need to let me help you."

"Jasmine, stop giving this young man a hard time," Lenora scolded as she walked up. "Let him patch up the burns you probably got from acting a fool."

"And what would you have me do?" Jasmine demanded. "My business was on fire." She waved a gauze-wrapped hand at Bertie. "And it's your fault."

"My fault?" Bertie asked.

"You're the one who told the whole town that I had something to do with those stupid notes," Jasmine said. "And not four hours later, someone tries to burn down my shop."

"I most certainly did not tell anyone that you were connected to those notes," Bertie said. "I was merely trying to show that almost anyone could be blamed. The whole exercise of trying to find links between anyone today and a poem written over a hundred years ago is ridiculous."

"Well, apparently *someone* took you seriously," Jasmine insisted.

"You think the fire was arson?" Jillian asked.

"My shop didn't just decide to up and burn," Jasmine snapped.

"It's an old building," Lenora said. "You've told me before that the wiring isn't great."

"Then why didn't it burn on a workday when I got all kinds of stuff plugged in and running? No, somebody tried to burn me out, all because Bertie Harper decided Poppy and I had something to do with those notes." Then Jasmine froze, her eyes wide. "Poppy. Somebody's gotta check on Poppy. If they went after me, maybe they went after my sister too." She pointed at Jillian. "You. Go see to my sister. Poppy's been sick, and I want to know she's all right."

"We could just call her," Lenora said, pulling out her cell phone again.

"No, you can't. Poppy went and canceled her cell phone plan. She read cell phones give you brain cancer, so she's going back to a landline. She just hasn't put hers in yet, which is just like her. She gets some fool idea and doesn't think it through. Now stop yapping and go get my sister."

"I'll go," Jillian said. "It makes sense to check on her. And she'll probably want to come see that you are okay."

"Okay?" Jasmine held up her wrapped hands. "Does this look okay to you? How am I supposed to cut hair when they got me trussed up like a mummy? *Okay.*" She harrumphed. "You go get my sister, before I decide you ain't got the sense for the job."

Jillian reminded herself that Jasmine had just been through a shock. "Fine, just tell me the address."

Savannah stepped up beside her and raised her hand. "I'll ride along. I know where Poppy lives."

"Good idea," Jillian said as they walked away from the ambulance and back toward the rubberneckers. "I appreciate having a little sane company. The whole town has been irrational lately."

"It's the weirdness of those notes. People like mysteries as a concept," Savannah said, "but not so much when they're dropped into their laps with no explanation. Those notes seem so irrational. That's what upsets everyone. People are scared of things they can't explain."

"There's nothing there to be scared of," Jillian said.

"That's just it. The very meaninglessness causes them to read all sorts of menace into it."

They made it through the crowd, and Jillian drove them back into town as Savannah gave her directions.

"How is it that you know where Poppy lives?" Jillian asked, then gave her friend a sidelong glance. "No, let me guess. You do her books?"

Savannah laughed. "I don't do the books for everyone in Moss Hollow. I went to a cookware party there once. It was before you moved back to town. Everyone who got their hair done that month ended up going to Poppy's party. Jasmine can be very convincing when she's got a hank of your hair and a pair of scissors. But I did end up buying some really nice baking sheets."

When they reached the small Craftsman-style cottage, Jillian admired the neatly tended gardens as they walked up the flagstone path from the street. "Poppy is certainly a talented gardener," Jillian said. Suddenly she stopped, peering at each flower bed.

"What?" Savannah asked.

"Do you see any fairies?" Jillian asked. "I distinctly remember someone saying Poppy had fairy silhouettes in her gardens."

"Yes, she normally does. I remember seeing them." Savannah looked around. "How odd."

"Maybe Jasmine told her to pull them up," Jillian suggested.

"That would go about as well as Bertie telling Cornelia to stop talking about the Belle Haven haint. Poppy would be more likely to buy more fairies and cram them in with the others."

"Maybe we should ask her about it." Jillian picked up her pace to the door and rang the bell. They waited but no one answered. She tried knocking, but still didn't get an answer.

"Maybe she's out in the backyard," Savannah suggested. "She might not be able to hear the door."

That seemed reasonable, but Jillian still felt increasingly worried. "Let's see if we can find her."

A tall, neatly trimmed hedge provided privacy to the backyard. An arched trellis and gate was the only passage through it. The gate hung open as they reached it.

"What on earth?" Savannah whispered.

Jillian followed her gaze through the gate to a pile of metal fairy silhouettes on long wires lying in the grass.

"Those are normally scattered in all the gardens," Savannah said. "Maybe you're right about hearing the things people said at church."

"Maybe." Jillian headed through the gate and into the backyard. A small flagstone patio took up the middle of the space. For a split second Jillian wondered at the blue floral cloth thrown on the patio. Then she saw it wasn't just a cloth. It was a robe.

And it was wrapped around Poppy.

4

By the time she finally got home to Belle Haven, Jillian felt totally numb. Poppy had been so still when they found her, and her skin was cold from lying on the ground. Jillian had actually thought the woman might be dead at first. She'd nearly wept from relief when Savannah found a pulse fluttering in Poppy's neck. Unfortunately, that was the last of their good news. Not even the ambulance crew had been able to bring Poppy around, and Jillian could tell by the grim faces on the ambulance team that Poppy's odds weren't good.

Jillian hadn't known Poppy, and now she wondered if she ever would. The image of the woman's still face wouldn't leave her thoughts.

Bertie met Jillian as soon as she came through the door of Belle Haven. "Come on into the kitchen," she said. "I've got the kettle on."

Jillian followed her grandmother, wondering how her feet had gotten so heavy. She felt as if days had passed since she was last home instead of mere hours. "How's Jasmine?"

"How would you be?" Bertie asked. "Her sister is in bad shape and her salon nearly burned down. It makes sense that Jasmine is a wreck, but Lenora is caring for her. This is a time for family, and Jasmine has a lot of family."

As Jillian shuffled into the kitchen, she saw Cornelia standing near a window, her arms full of cat. Possum wasn't fond of being carried around by anyone but Cornelia. "Are you all right?" Cornelia asked.

Jillian sat down heavily on one of the kitchen stools. "I'm just numb. You'd think I'd get used to this kind of shock. It's hardly the first time I've found someone unconscious. I think it's because she was outside, and I honestly thought she was dead at first."

Bertie opened the cupboard and took down a mug. "You don't want to get used to something like this. It should always be shocking and horrible. It proves you're human."

"What happened?" Cornelia asked as she walked closer, hugging the cat like a security blanket. "Was it an accident? Did Poppy fall or something?"

"I don't know," Jillian said. "There were no injuries that Savannah or I could see. She just wouldn't wake up."

"Poppy's been sick," Bertie said as she poured hot water over a tea bag. "And she was always a little frail. Diabetic, as I remember, and maybe something else. Cornelia, you're better at remembering things like that. What ailed the girl?"

"I remember the diabetic part," Cornelia said, "but it does seem like there was something with her heart when she and Jasmine were kids."

"That sounds right." Bertie pushed the mug over to Jillian. "So it was likely that whatever happened is related to her being sickly."

Jillian stared into the slowly swirling tea. "I imagine so. Though the timing couldn't possibly have been worse."

"There's never a good time for something like this," Cornelia said firmly.

Jillian nodded in agreement and took a sip of her tea. The hot liquid helped warm her. She hadn't noticed how cold she felt until then. She leaned back in the chair and soaked up the comfort. "What about the fire? Was it accidental?"

Bertie shrugged as she put the lid back on the tea canister. "Jasmine doesn't think so, but I think it's too soon for a determination. I imagine we'll hear something next week."

Jillian sipped again. Something about the heat and being in the kitchen with her family finally began to unclench some of the knots inside her. She thought again about the pile of fairy silhouettes lying on the grass inside Poppy's garden gate. "I wonder why she pulled them up."

"Pulled what up?" Bertie asked.

"The fairies," Jillian said. "You remember at church how someone said Poppy's gardens were full of fairies."

"They were," Cornelia said. "I've seen them. Poppy is mad about fairies. She's in the garden club. Well, not exactly in it. She comes to the meetings now and then." Cornelia smiled slightly. "She told us she wasn't a joiner. But she invited us out to see her garden. She really did a lovely job, though I thought the fairies were a little overdone."

"When Savannah and I got to Poppy's house, I noticed there were no fairies anywhere. When we didn't get an answer to the doorbell and went around back, we found a pile of the fairy silhouettes on stakes on the grass near the hedge. I guess Poppy had pulled them all up."

"Why would she do that?" Bertie asked.

Cornelia put Possum down, and the cat rushed over to stare at the fridge. His tail twitched in annoyance when no one opened it and gave him his favorite treat—bacon. "Maybe Jasmine told her to," Cornelia suggested, "after those people were acting so strangely at church."

"How? She couldn't have called her," Jillian said. "Jasmine said Poppy didn't have a phone."

"Maybe she told her at church," Bertie said. "I don't remember seeing Poppy this morning, but I wasn't watching for her either."

Cornelia walked over to the fridge, and Possum rubbed against her ankles, meowing. "She might not have been there. Jasmine said she'd been sick. Stop your hollering, Raymond." Cornelia often addressed the cat by her late husband's name, convinced that somehow the cat channeled his spirit—or something like that. Jillian wasn't really clear on the particulars.

Bertie poked Jillian in the arm. "Don't go making this into one of your investigations. Sounds like whatever happened to Poppy was due to her frailty, and I expect they'll find out that Jasmine's fire was bad wiring or some such. That was an old building her salon was in. She's lucky it didn't burn on a business day. No need to borrow trouble when we don't have the facts."

"Of course." But Jillian suspected she didn't need to borrow trouble. She had a feeling trouble had already arrived.

Gossip at the bakery the next morning was certainly full of doom, and since Maggie was still sick, Jillian had no way to dodge it.

"I heard someone bashed poor Poppy in the head," Mrs. Gantry said as she clutched her purse in white-knuckled hands. "And everyone is saying it was the person who wrote those awful notes."

"Poppy wasn't bashed in the head, and I don't think she ever got one of the notes either," Jillian said calmly as she slid a cinnamon roll into a small pastry box. Poppy didn't have a business, but Jillian wasn't totally sure that the notes were only to business owners. "Did you get a note, Mrs. Gantry?"

Mrs. Gantry shook her head, making her pin curls bounce. "No. But if Poppy didn't either, maybe the attacker is only going after the people who didn't get notes?" Her eyes widened as she spoke. "Maybe we're all in danger."

"No one bashed Poppy," Jillian said. "I saw her. No sign of bashing. I think maybe she just got sick."

Mrs. Gantry leaned close to Jillian. "But would you tell us if she was bashed?"

"I wouldn't lie about it," Jillian said, feeling the ends of her temper fray, but managing to keep her voice level. "Now, may I get you anything else today?"

As she made change for the nosy woman, Jillian glanced over at Stewie with his nose buried in the Atlanta newspaper. She envied his ability to take out his hearing aids and shut out all the crazy gossip whirling around him.

The bell over the door jingled to announce another customer. Jasmine stormed over to the counter. Instead of her usual bright clothes, she wore a simple navy dress, but her mood was clearly more volatile than somber. "You!" she snapped at Jillian. "I want to talk to you, and I don't have much time. Now."

Jillian blinked in surprise. "Hold on." She slipped into the kitchen. "Lenora, your cousin is here. She wants to chat privately with me. Can you either ward her off or watch the front so I can see what she wants?"

Lenora sighed. "Jasmine isn't thinking straight right now. You go talk to her. I'll watch the front. Take her up to the apartment. You can have some privacy that way."

Not long before Jillian returned to Moss Hollow, Lenora had sold her house and moved into the small apartment over the bakery. It was a huge help for Bertie to have someone there for emergencies, and Lenora said she liked the apartment far better than having all the chores that come with a house and garden. The apartment was small, but charming.

Jasmine followed Jillian up to the apartment without comment. She sat perched at the edge of a small rocking chair in Lenora's room. Despite her previous rush to talk to Jillian, she seemed almost hesitant now. "Poppy still hasn't woke up. The doctors said her flu messed up her sugar somehow, which put a strain on her heart. Sounds like guessing to me. And that's what the fire marshal is doing about the fire at my place too." She nervously smoothed her dress over her knees with her bandaged hands. "And I don't like the shifty way the man was peering at me, like I might set fire to my own salon."

"I'm sure he's just considering all the options."

"The only *option* as far as I'm concerned is that someone set fire to my shop!" She poked at the bandages on her right hand, her eyes still downcast. "But I didn't come here to talk about the fire marshal's foolishness."

"Why are you here, Jasmine?" Jillian asked softly.

The other woman met her gaze, and Jillian was struck by how tired Jasmine looked. The little woman was usually a bundle of energy. "Poppy and I don't get along much. We don't fight really. We just don't have much in common. We live right here in the same town, and I don't think we saw each other more than twice a year outside of church."

"Family can be challenging," Jillian said.

"When we were little, Poppy was always so frail. She got sick all the time, and it seemed like she got all the attention. That's probably why I got so loud and bossy. I was just trying to get some notice, you know?"

Jillian nodded.

"But it wasn't Poppy's fault. Some folks, they're just not strong." She sighed deeply. "The doctor told me Poppy might not wake up. They're doing what they can, but they're making me no promises. I knew she had the flu, and I can't believe I didn't even go over and check on her. But she was always sick. I couldn't go over every time."

"You couldn't have known," Jillian said gently.

Jasmine continued to run her hands over her dress hem. "Yeah, I couldn't have known. Unless I'd been a good sister and kept up. The doctors think Poppy just got confused, being sick and all, and walked outside and collapsed. Being out in the cold didn't do her any good. Doctor said it might have been the one thing too many. We just have to wait and see." Her voice dropped to a whisper. "Wait and see."

"I'm sorry."

"Everyone is. I don't know. Maybe Poppy just wandered outside. Maybe she was trying to get help. Maybe someone chased her. I'd like to find out though. These last few days—they haven't been normal, you know? Those notes. Bonnie's crazy theory. The scene at the church. The fire. Poppy. I need to know how much of that is tied together."

"Maybe none of it," Jillian said. "You said the fire marshal has been looking at you funny. Have you heard anything specific about the fire?"

Jasmine folded her bandaged hands on her lap. "Someone left a curling iron plugged in, and it fell into a wastebasket. That's what the fire marshal said, but I know curling irons can be dangerous. Every one of us at the salon knows that. We're careful with them. None of my girls would have left a curling iron plugged in on Saturday when they left."

"So you don't believe it was an accident?" Jillian asked.

"I don't know," Jasmine said. "But the insurance company is squawking about it like they think I did it on purpose to get the insurance money. I'll have to wait until they finish their investigation before I can remodel and get the business open again." She held up her bandaged hands. "Not that I could cut hair right now anyway."

"How did you find out about the fire anyway?" Jillian asked. "You don't live at the salon."

"Just luck, I reckon. Bonnie's ranting at the church made me nervous. After I ate some lunch, I couldn't get it out of my head, so I went over to the salon to check on everything. I thought it would make me feel better. I parked around back and came in the back door. I heard a crash out front, and when I got there, the fire was already going pretty well. I tried to put it out with the fire extinguisher we have, and I was making some headway until it caught a cardboard box of hair spray cans." She sighed. "Once the cans started exploding, I was lucky to get out of there." She held up a hand. "It had already heated up the doorknob a good bit."

Jillian winced. "I'm glad you got out."

"Yeah." Jasmine held up her bandages. "At least this is temporary." She peered into Jillian's eyes. "Will you do it? Will you try to find out what happened?"

"I don't know what you want. It sounds like you know what happened."

"I know a curling iron started a fire," Jasmine said. "And the crash I heard might have been the curling iron just happening to fall. But what if it wasn't? And maybe Poppy got confused and walked outside to fall down, but what if there's more going on, and no one is looking?"

"I don't know if I'll find anything," Jillian said softly.

"That's fine," Jasmine said. "Just promise me you'll try."

Jillian nodded. "I'll try."

The mixture of relief and sorrow on Jasmine's face made Jillian feel like she'd done the right thing. She certainly hoped so, because she suspected she'd just opened a can of worms that wasn't going to make anyone else particularly happy.

5

"I appreciate you wanting to help Jasmine," Lenora said as she cut butter into dough. "But I wish she could just let it go. Poppy's condition isn't her fault, and that's the truth."

"Guilt doesn't always care about truth," Bertie said from the table where she was twisting balls of dough into neat little knot rolls.

Jillian sighed as she picked up a piping bag full of buttercream frosting. She'd been glad when Celia showed up to take over the front, but now she was feeling nearly as grilled in the kitchen as she had when facing the nosy customers. "I'm trying to do the right thing, that's all."

Lenora punched down the dough. "I know, but I worry that humoring Jasmine is just going to encourage her to hold onto the idea that more is going on than just a sick woman getting sicker. The family is trying to help her get her head on straight, but it's not easy."

Jillian paused in piping the frosting onto cupcakes. "I know Poppy's condition isn't Jasmine's fault, and I told Jasmine that. But maybe it'll help to know someone is checking into it. Someone is poking around and asking questions."

"I would rather that someone wasn't you," Bertie told her.

"*I* would rather it wasn't me. But Jasmine asked, and I didn't have the heart to refuse."

"Just be careful." Lenora picked up a rolling pin and began to flatten the buttery dough. "And please don't say anything to Jasmine to worry her or get her riled up. You know how she is."

"She didn't seem very riled when I talked to her." Jillian carefully piped a spiral of buttercream on top of the cupcake. "In fact, she wasn't anything like her normal self. She was more . . .

defeated. Like she'd given up." She stopped again and met Bertie's gaze, then Lenora's. "If I can do anything to help, I have to do it."

"So what are you going to do?" Bertie asked. "None of this makes any sense at all. I don't see how you're going to figure out *who* to ask, much less *what* to ask."

"I'm going over to take a peek at the salon at the end of the day," Jillian said. "The fire chief has declared the building is structurally secure, and Jasmine gave me the keys to get in and look around."

Lenora paused in her rolling. "What do you think you'll find?"

"I'm hoping I'll know when I see it."

"I suppose that's as good a strategy as any." Bertie lifted the tray of rolls and carried it over to the oven, ending the discussion.

Nothing more was said about Jillian's plan for the next hour, but Jillian was surprised when her grandmother pulled her aside. "Give Savannah a call and see if she can go over to the salon with you. I don't like you going by yourself."

"Okay, sounds like a good idea," Jillian agreed. "I'll see if she's available at closing."

"You don't have to wait. Call her now and go. Lenora and I can handle finishing up here. I reckon you're right, Jasmine needs you to do this." Then Bertie's tone became stern. "But if Savannah can't go with you, see if Hunter can. I don't want you going by yourself. It might be dangerous."

"The fire marshal said the building was still structurally sound," Jillian said.

"That's good. I still don't want you going alone. If Hunter can't go, maybe Laura Lee can. Just go with someone."

Jillian realized her grandmother was truly worried, so she agreed. Luckily she didn't have to call all over town. Savannah was happy to help. "Are you leaving now?" she asked. "I'm coming from a different direction so it makes more sense if I meet you there."

"Good plan. I'll be out of here in a few minutes." Jillian slid the hairnet off her head and headed out into the customer area. She'd parked down the street in the tourist lot instead of behind the bakery, hoping to do a little shopping after work. Most of the businesses were keeping later hours to lure in customers for Christmas shopping. Unfortunately, her Christmas shopping would probably have to be put on hold for a while.

Celia caught her before she could slip out. "Are you leaving?"

"Bertie gave me the rest of the day off," Jillian said. "I'm on an errand for Jasmine."

Celia's expression darkened. "Auntie Jasmine is pretty wrecked."

"She is."

"Before you leave, do you have a minute?" Celia asked. "There are no customers right now, and I need to tell you something."

"Sure, but can it wait?" Jillian asked. "I'm supposed to meet Savannah over at the Clip & Curl."

Celia shifted nervously, then shrugged. "Sure. It can wait. Maybe I could come out to Belle Haven? I have a friend, and she kinda needs to talk to someone. I thought you could help."

Jillian almost groaned. She liked Celia and generally liked teenagers, but she'd never seen herself in the big-sister confidant role. Plus, if Celia's friend was in some kind of trouble, Jillian didn't think she'd win any points when she insisted on contacting parents. "Are you sure I'm the right person to talk to? Seems like Lenora would be better, since she's family."

Celia shook her head vehemently. "No, but it's okay. You don't want to, I understand."

Jillian felt a pang of guilt as the teenager tried to backpedal. *Great role model I am.* "No, no, it's fine. You come out to the house after work, and we'll talk. I just have to run right now."

Celia nodded, not saying anything else. As Jillian walked down the sidewalk to the tourist parking lot, she tried to imagine what kinds of things a teenager might want to have a private talk about. None of the possibilities that came to mind sounded promising. Maybe Celia and her friend wanted to talk about colleges. Jillian hadn't done any recent research, but she knew of some fine schools, so she held onto that hope and picked up her pace.

As she walked past the library, she saw Josi Rosenschein standing next to the group of cozy chairs near the tall front windows that let readers enjoy the outside while they read. Josi spotted Jillian and waved. Then she quickly held up one finger, gesturing to say she was coming out to talk to Jillian.

Why does everyone want to talk to me when I'm on my way somewhere? She smiled at Josi and nodded, hoping whatever her friend needed wouldn't take too long. The library door swung open and Josi trotted out. She hadn't even bothered to put a sweater on, so Jillian knew Josi wouldn't keep her long. It wasn't exactly frigid out, but the breeze was chilly and Jillian was glad of her light jacket. "Hi Josi!"

"Hi." Josi glanced around, putting Jillian in mind of someone in an old spy film making sure they weren't being overheard. Considering they were standing in front of the window where four people were sitting and watching them, this wasn't exactly a clandestine meeting.

"Did you need something?" Jillian asked.

"I heard you were investigating the notes," Josi said. "The ones with the poetry."

"Did the library get one?" Jillian asked. "I didn't see you at the council meeting."

"We got one, but I didn't see any point in the council meeting. It was a quote from a poem, not a terrorist threat."

"True." Jillian waited for Josi to get around to asking whatever was on her mind.

"I can't tell you," Josi said finally.

"You can't tell me what's on your mind?" Jillian said, totally confused.

"No. I can't tell you who might have checked out books on Christina Rossetti or Victorian poetry or anything like that," Josi said. "It would violate patron privacy."

Jillian raised her eyebrows at the librarian in surprise. "I actually never thought about asking. The poem is readily available online. I don't see why anyone would have to check out a book." She raised her eyebrows. "Why? Do you know something?"

"I just told you," Josi insisted. "I can't tell you."

"Right. Okay, I won't ask," Jillian said. "But if you could tell me—which you can't—would you have something to tell me?" Just saying the words made Jillian realize how ridiculous it sounded.

"Maybe, yeah," Josi said, dropping her voice to barely a whisper. "But if I could tell you, I'd say that any person who might have been researching Rossetti would never do anything like burn down a store or attack anyone."

"Okay," Jillian said. "That's good to know."

Josi stood straighter, as if the conversation had gotten something off her chest. If it did, Jillian couldn't imagine what. It had been one of the most confusing conversations she'd ever had, which was saying a lot considering Cornelia was her aunt.

"I have to get back to work." Josi smiled. "Good luck."

"Thanks." Jillian watched her friend hurry back into the library. Then with a shrug, she walked the rest of the way to her car. Despite the chill in the breeze, the sun on her car had heated the inside, so Jillian drove to the salon with the windows cracked.

She wasn't surprised to see Savannah's car already parked in front of the closed salon. Savannah stood leaning on the car's bumper and texting on her phone. She looked up as Jillian pulled in beside her and waved.

Jillian hopped out. "Sorry to make you wait."

"No problem," Savannah said. "It gave me a chance to text James. He's at work, so I didn't want to call."

"I'm not keeping you from meeting him?" Jillian asked. "I don't want to get in the way of wedding planning."

"No. He's coming over for dinner after work, and I already have a nice cassoulet in the slow cooker. All I need to do when I get home is make some cheesy rosemary biscuits."

"Sounds delicious. I bet he's glad he proposed." Jillian reached into the pocket of her white bakery pants and pulled out a key. "Let's go poke around."

As soon as she unlocked the door and they stepped in, Savannah whistled. "I'm not sure all white is the best clothing choice for poking around in here." She gestured toward Jillian's bakery clothes.

"The decor *is* a little on the soggy-ash side," Jillian said. "But the good thing about this outfit is I can bleach just about anything out of it." She let her gaze sweep across the room. "I think we should start near the back and work our way forward."

As they made their way slowly through the room, Jillian wondered how much stuff Jasmine would need to replace before she could reopen. Jillian could see that the actual structure didn't seem to be damaged beneath the surface. The walls were smoke-streaked, and a half-wall near the salon chairs was definitely scorched. One of the chairs was probably a total ruin, as was the shelf behind it.

"I wonder if this is where it started," Jillian said. "It seems to have the worst damage."

"Seems likely," Savannah agreed. She pushed some of the burned bits on the floor with her shoe. "It's hard to tell what all this was. I just see some twisted metal."

"Jasmine said the fire made some hair spray cans explode," Jillian said. "Maybe that's shrapnel."

"Jasmine's lucky she wasn't hurt much more seriously," Savannah said.

Jillian walked to the back of the room where Jasmine would have come in from the rear door and methodically scanned the room. She saw the chair closest to the back door was mostly untouched by the fire, though everything was soggy with the water used to extinguish the fire, and the trash can at that station had been upset. "I wonder how that happened."

Savannah was squatting and poking at a pile of blackened bits on the floor. "What? The fire?"

"No, I wonder what knocked this trash can over. Nothing else over here is messed up."

Savannah stood up and joined her. "Maybe it fell over when the firemen sprayed it. Those hoses pack a wallop."

"But wouldn't they have been standing near the front of the building? My guess is this can was knocked over from back here. Like someone tripped over it."

"Maybe Jasmine did," Savannah said. "She must have been shook up to come into the room and see it on fire."

"That would make sense," Jillian agreed. "Though it's her shop, so you'd think she wouldn't fall over things in it."

Savannah laughed. "Then I better not tell you the number of times I've tripped over things in my cottage, especially first thing in the morning."

Jillian knew it was a reasonable theory. Still, she walked closer to the station. Mostly it wasn't in bad shape. A puddle of water lay in the seat of the salon chair and more puddles filled the wells where the stylist kept combs and curling irons. Then Jillian saw something peeking out from behind the chair—a whiteboard.

She pulled the whiteboard out from behind the chair. Most of whatever had once been written on it was nothing but smears, blasted away by the force of the firehose. But the chair had shielded a small area.

"Savannah," Jillian said, "look at this."

She held the board so her friend could read it. Only three words were still readable. The first was *know* and the last two were *or else.*

"Or else what?" Savannah asked softly.

"Good question. And I think we'd better find the answer."

6

Jillian snapped photos of the whiteboard with her phone, though she didn't think she was likely to gain more from the message with further study. She stood in the middle of the char and muck, and wondered what to do next. Usually she had *some* idea. Someone to talk to. Someplace to poke around. But she stood studying the whiteboard, wondering what it meant and who to ask about it.

"Jillian?" Savannah said.

Jillian jumped, startled. She'd forgotten she wasn't alone. "Yes?"

"You seemed lost for a minute there."

Jillian studied the whiteboard again. "I don't know what to do. Jasmine asked me to help. Does this mean she's right? Was someone in here? Did someone start the fire?" She gazed around the room and tried to put together what she saw.

"That certainly isn't something you'd expect to find on a whiteboard of a salon, but who knows? Maybe Jasmine was telling a stylist she needed to know the names of her clients or else. I can imagine scenarios where those words fit."

Jillian nodded slowly. "So the first thing I need to do is find out if someone in the salon wrote that." She took a deep breath, feeling better suddenly. She smiled slightly. "I have my next step."

Savannah pulled out her phone to check the time. "I don't have to head home quite yet. You want to drive over to Jasmine's house? I could come with."

"Thanks. Let me call and see if she's home. She could be at the hospital."

Jasmine lived in one half of a white ranch-style duplex. At a glance, it was clear Jasmine had a totally different sense of style from whoever lived in the other half. The built-in planter that ran the length of Jasmine's small porch was filled with yucca plants and decorative rocks, and her porch held a single rocking chair and a string of white lights wrapped around the porch railing. The other porch planter was a riot of color, including two plastic flamingos, presently wearing Santa hats. The porch was bare of furniture, but held a large plastic Santa whose suit had faded to a chalky pink. Shiny plastic ornaments dangled from the gold garland wrapped around the porch.

Jasmine came out to her porch as they headed up the front walk. "I'm so glad you're here. Come in and open a jar for me, please?" She held up her hands. "These are useless right now."

"Happy to be of service," Savannah said.

"Your neighbor certainly likes color," Jillian said as they followed her inside.

Jasmine rolled her eyes. "That's my aunt. I'm considering kidnapping that Santa in the middle of the night and carrying it to the dump, but I'm afraid to imagine what she'd replace it with. She's at the hospital with Poppy right now. When I drove back to the hospital after talking to you, she practically shoved me into my car and made me come home."

Jillian thought Jasmine looked much better than she had at the bakery. Had knowing someone was trying to figure out the fire and her sister's mishap given her this much relief? If so, Jillian was glad she'd taken it on.

As Savannah wrestled the jar of pickles, Jasmine aimed a sharp glare at Jillian, who was startled by how much she resembled her cousin Lenora in that moment. "You been to the salon?"

"I did. I have something to show you." She brought up the photo of the whiteboard on her phone. "Did you write that on the board?"

Jasmine read it, then shook her head. "No. That's Ayesha's station. You should ask her to be sure." She frowned at Jillian. "It's a weird thing to put on the board. You think it's related to the fire?"

"I don't know," Jillian said. "It's a long shot."

Savannah stepped over to the sink to run hot water on the stubborn jar lid. "Did you notice the sign when you came into the salon?"

"No. The fire was kind of attention-grabbing."

Savannah handed her the open jar with a triumphant smile.

Jillian leaned against the counter, while Jasmine poked around in a drawer for a fork. "I noticed a trash can at Ayesha's station was overturned on the floor. Did you happen to see that?"

Jasmine's eyes widened. "I did see that. I totally forgot about that. I almost tripped over it. I remember wondering if that was the crash I heard."

"What would make the trash can fall over?" Jillian asked.

"Other than someone knocking it over, I don't know." Jasmine set the pickle jar and fork on the counter. "I'm being a terrible hostess. Can I get y'all something? I have a pitcher of sweet tea that Lenora made for me."

"That would be nice," Jillian said. "I can still taste char."

Jasmine walked to her fridge and winced as she hefted the pitcher. Savannah quickly took it from her and poured the drinks. She handed a glass to Jasmine, who thanked her glumly. "I hate being helpless."

"Is there anything we can do to help?" Savannah asked.

"You did it," Jasmine said. "You opened my pickles and you poured me some tea." Then her expression grew more serious. "And I appreciate what you're doing about the salon too. You got any theories?"

"I might," Jillian said. "Once I know for sure if the message on the whiteboard is as strange as it seems."

"Then let's give Ayesha a call." Jasmine walked over to her small sitting room and picked up her phone from a table. She swiped through her contacts with the one finger not wrapped in gauze and quickly made the call. Ayesha answered quickly, and Jillian sipped her tea as Jasmine responded to what were clearly some sympathetic remarks. Then Jasmine got to the point. "I'm going to put you on speakerphone. I've got Jillian Green and Savannah Cantrell here. They're checking into the fire for me."

"Checking into the fire?" Ayesha echoed. "What are you talking about? I thought the fire marshal said it was a curling iron left plugged in."

"Yeah, and who among us is fool enough to leave a curling iron plugged in?" Jasmine asked. "Nobody has been using that station regular since Ginny left. So who do you reckon left it plugged in?"

"I don't know," Ayesha said. "But why would you ask folks to poke around in it?"

"'Cause it doesn't make sense. And I need some things to make sense right now. Now stop arguing and answer a question."

"What?"

Jasmine held the phone toward Jillian. "Ayesha," Jillian said. "Did you have a note on your whiteboard with the words 'or else' in it?"

"Or else?" Ayesha said. "Why would I write something like that? I use that board to keep up with my clients every day. If it had anything on it, it would have been names. Not foolishness."

Jasmine thanked Ayesha and ended the call. "Fine. So now you know. That message wasn't normal. So what's your theory?"

"I wonder if someone was in the salon," Jillian said. "Maybe writing on the whiteboard about the notes everyone's been getting. And the person heard you. So whoever it was ran, knocking over the trash can and maybe knocking the curling iron into the other trash can as well."

"But the curling iron wasn't plugged in," Jasmine insisted. "It wouldn't have been. So whoever wrote that note started the fire on purpose. And I want to know who that was. And maybe burning down my salon wasn't enough for them. Maybe they went after Poppy too."

"I don't know about anyone hurting Poppy, but I did wonder about someone having been in Poppy's yard," Jillian said. "When Savannah and I went to her house, all her garden fairies were gone. We found them in a pile right inside the backyard hedge."

Jasmine raised a bandaged hand to her mouth. "Oh my." She slowly sank into the sitting room chair. "Poppy wouldn't have pulled up those fairies. She loves the stupid things. They were mostly presents. That's why she had so many. Everyone in the family knows what to give Poppy." Her brown eyes filled with tears. "If the fairies were pulled up, Poppy didn't do it. And if someone pulled up Poppy's fairies, did they stop there?" She stared at Jillian. "Did someone hurt my sister?"

"I don't know," Jillian said quietly.

"It doesn't have to mean that," Savannah insisted. "Someone could have pulled up the fairies long before Poppy came outside, especially since your sister wasn't feeling well. It wouldn't have been hard for someone to quietly gather up all the fairies as some kind of message."

"Unless Poppy caught the person," Jasmine said. "And they chased her until she collapsed."

"It's too soon to jump to those kinds of conclusions," Savannah said.

"I don't think it's too early," Jasmine snapped. "It was Bonnie Steck. She was rabid over those notes. And then Bertie sent her sniffing around Poppy and me. *She* did it. I can feel her nastiness all over it. She practically threatened me at church."

"Bonnie was upset about the notes," Jillian agreed. "But so were you."

"Well, I certainly didn't burn up my own salon or vandalize my sister's yard and maybe attack her," Jasmine snapped. "This is connected with those notes. I don't know how, but I know it is. And when I find out what's going on, someone is going to pay!"

Jillian and Savannah tried to calm Jasmine, but neither could really blame her for being upset. She was grieving for her business and her sister's condition, and grief wasn't always rational. Jillian just hoped she could find some answers before Jasmine rode that grief into even more trouble.

As they left Jasmine's house, Jillian thanked Savannah again for coming along with her. "I'm always happy to join in," Savannah said. "You know that."

"I know," Jillian agreed, "but I don't always understand it. I certainly have dragged you into some awful things."

"That's what friends are for," Savannah said. "Plus, we've also had some interesting adventures." She gave Jillian a hug. "I have to run and feed a hungry man. Let me know if you need a partner in further sleuthing."

"I promise I will."

As Jillian drove home, she mulled over what she knew. She suspected that Jasmine was right, that the break-in at the salon and Poppy's fairies being moved were related to the notes. But she wasn't sure exactly what the goal of the break-in or the vandalism had been. Were they pranks that had spun out of control? Or had they been intentional?

She also thought about her odd conversation with Josi. The librarian clearly knew more than she felt she could say, and the knowledge was weighing heavily on her. "It's like I'm trying to see through a fogged-up window," Jillian complained aloud. "I know there's something there, but I can't tell what it is."

To take her mind off her frustration, Jillian made an effort to admire the Christmas decorations she saw at some of the houses she passed. It was still early, with Thanksgiving barely behind them, so she knew more decorations would be appearing before Christmas arrived. Still, she saw wreaths on the doors of some of the older homes, and even a few Christmas trees through the windows.

She was reminded suddenly of her grandfather. Grandpa Jack had loved Christmas, and he would have covered Belle Haven in colored lights if Bertie had let him. She had declared it a waste of money and electricity, and had limited him to greenery. So he'd sneak away after supper and drive over to pick up Jillian. Then they would drive around all the neighborhoods and admire the bright colors of the blinking lights. Sure, some of the displays were tacky, but that just added to the fun.

She was still feeling a little nostalgic as she pulled around and parked under the porte cochere at Belle Haven. She let herself in through the side entrance and walked to the kitchen.

Cornelia was bent over in front of the oven, pulling out a pan of cookies. The aroma of warm chocolate filled the kitchen.

Celia Ryan perched on one of the kitchen stools, dunking a cookie into a glass of milk. Beside her was another teenager Jillian didn't recognize. The girl had long, straight brown hair pulled back into a single braid and a heart-shaped face with a spray of freckles across her nose. Jillian almost groaned. She'd completely forgotten Celia was bringing a friend over for some kind of big-sister talk.

Jillian forced a smile on her face. "Something smells delicious."

"Chocolate shortbread with lots of butter," Cornelia said. "The girls are helping me work out a recipe. I'm making them for the Christmas bazaar at church."

"This recipe is perfect," Celia said.

"Perfecto," her friend agreed.

"Well, at the risk of spoiling my supper, I might have to try one myself." Jillian walked over and took a cookie from one of the baking sheets. The shortbread broke easily and melted in her mouth, leaving behind hints of chocolate and butter. "Oh wow. We should add these to the selection at the bakery."

Cornelia beamed at her. "It's a nice dunking cookie too. I ate one with a cup of coffee."

"Well, if we have any left, I'll have to try that after supper." Jillian smiled at Celia and her friend. "I'm sorry I kept you guys waiting. I got caught up in an errand."

"We're not sorry," Celia said.

"Miss Cornelia's cookies were worth the wait," her friend said. She smiled a little shyly at Jillian. "I'm Sidney."

Jillian offered her hand. "Pleased to meet you, Sidney. I'm Jillian."

Sidney shook her hand. "I know. Celia has told me a lot about you."

Jillian gave Celia a glance. "Only good things, I hope."

"Oh yes." Sidney gave her a wide-eyed expression of sincerity as she pushed an escaped strand of hair behind one ear. "She says you're really smart."

"Oh." *That* was a surprise. "Celia said you had something you wanted to talk to me about?"

Sidney shifted on her seat and stared down into her glass of milk. Celia gave her an elbow to the ribs. "Tell her."

Sidney shot Celia a glare, then peeked sideways at Cornelia. Jillian's great-aunt took the hint immediately. "Well, that was the last batch of cookies. I'm going to go see what Bertie wants for supper." She marched out of the kitchen, heading toward Bertie's room.

Jillian sat down on one of the kitchen stools and folded her forearms on the counter. "It's just us now. What did you want to tell me?"

"I've done something awful," Sidney said softly. "Really awful."

Jillian suddenly had an uncomfortable feeling she was about to hear something better saved for Sidney's parents. "Are you sure I'm the right person for this?"

Both the girls nodded, their expressions grave.

Jillian sighed. "Okay. I'm listening. What did you do that was so awful?"

Tears filled Sidney's eyes, and she answered in a choked voice. "I think I killed someone."

Jillian stared at the crying girl in shock. "I don't understand. Do you mean you had a car accident? Something like that?"

Sidney shook her head hard, sending her braid swinging.

"She didn't mean any harm," Celia insisted, then she nudged her friend. "And Poppy's not dead. Stop being a drama queen."

"Poppy? You did something to Poppy? I think I need a lot more information." Jillian reached out and put her hand on top of Sidney's forearm. "I can't help you if I don't know what's going on."

"I can tell her," Celia offered, putting her own hand on Sidney's shoulder.

Sidney shook her head, then hiccupped as she fought for control of her emotions. Finally she picked up the napkin in front of her and wiped at her eyes. "I'm sorry." Her voice was still thick. "I didn't intend to fall apart."

"It sounds like you've been carrying something pretty heavy," Jillian said gently. "Why don't you tell me about it?"

Sidney nodded, but Jillian still had to wait for the girl to take a few deep breaths. "I'm a senior, and I wanted to do an independent study project. It's good for my college applications." She paused again for more slow breaths.

Jillian waited without asking any more questions. She had no idea how a high school project had anything to do with Poppy's condition, but clearly they were going to take the long way around on this explanation.

"I was watching old TV shows," Sidney said. "I saw this *Twilight Zone* episode about these people who lived on the same street.

A few weird things happened, and they turned on each other. I thought that was stupid. I didn't think that would really happen."

Celia cut in. "She talked about it at *every* lunch break for weeks."

"Not weeks," Sidney protested.

"Weeks!" Celia insisted.

"And?" Jillian prompted.

"And I decided to do a senior project to prove that people in real life don't act like that. Something weird that doesn't threaten anyone wouldn't make small town people go crazy." Her voice broke at the end.

Jillian waited for the girl to regain control, but she had a pretty good idea what was coming. "You sent the notes," she said after Sidney seemed more composed.

Sidney nodded and her eyes flooded again. "They were just quotes from a poem! It's not even a violent poem. It's like a fairy tale."

Jillian nodded. "I know. I've read it. Why send them to businesses?"

"Because it would be easier to keep track of the response. I could actually go to the businesses and observe." She shrugged. "And it wouldn't be trespassing. I wanted to make sure I didn't do anything illegal." At the word *illegal*, she sobbed.

Jillian watched the sobbing teenager. She wasn't sure what to do with this information. If it became public knowledge, the girl's life was going to be really rough. She knew how awful it felt when everyone in Moss Hollow was mad at you. Someone needed to get the word out that the notes were benign, but it had to be someone who would keep Sidney's secret. Then an idea hit her.

"I think I know exactly the right person to help with this," she said.

Sidney blinked. "Who?"

"Pastor Keith. He has a platform to spread the word that the notes weren't meant to hurt anyone. He can keep your identity confidential. And he's a great person to talk to."

Sidney nodded. "Pastor Keith is nice. But won't he hate me? Someone might die because of my notes."

"It's his job *not* to hate. Besides, your notes probably didn't have anything to do with Poppy's condition," Jillian said. "She'd been sick. But I think we do need to keep your name out of this so you don't end up being blamed, at least by some people."

"You don't think she'll get kicked out of school?" Celia asked, making her friend sob again.

Jillian tried for a reassuring smile. "I think we need to take this one step at a time. Let me call Pastor Keith and see if he can spare us some time. We need to get the town calmed down as soon as possible."

Before she made the call, she had a thought. "Did you get the Rossetti poem from a book at the library?"

Sidney bobbed her head.

Well, that explains the conversation with Josi. Jillian almost smiled as she thought about Josi's earnest face. *No wonder she didn't want to say who'd checked out the book.*

After making the call, Jillian went in search of Cornelia to let her know she was driving over to the church to help the girls. She was also glad to give Celia and Sidney a moment alone. She couldn't imagine what Sidney must be going through. Jillian remembered her own teen years. Sometimes she'd had some pretty bad ideas, but nothing that had ever had quite so much impact.

She found Cornelia in the living room with her shoes kicked off and curled up on the sofa. She held a book in her lap and Possum lay pressed against Cornelia's hip with one paw resting on the book as if to be certain his beloved human didn't forget he was right there. Cornelia looked up as Jillian walked in. "Are the girls gone?"

"No, we're all going over to talk to Pastor Keith."

Cornelia raised her eyebrows. "It's a spiritual problem? And Celia thought you were the best person to talk to about it?"

"Hey, I'm a spiritual person," Jillian said. "But it's not a spiritual problem. It is something she told me in confidence though, so that's all I'm saying. I just wanted to tell you I'm leaving. Don't wait supper on me."

"All right." Cornelia raised her book again. "But don't forget to eat. You skip too many meals when you're caught up in these things. You're as bad as Bertie. She only wants a sandwich. What kind of dinner is that?"

Jillian leaned over to give her aunt a peck on the cheek. "I'll be sure to eat something."

Cornelia sniffed. "Be sure that you do. And maybe when you get home, you can tell me what's going on."

"I don't know," Jillian said. "It's not my story to tell."

Cornelia buried her nose in her book, pointedly shutting Jillian out.

With a sigh, Jillian headed back to the kitchen. The girls both appeared to be considerably more composed. "Let's get going," she said.

Pastor Keith was every bit as kind and consoling as Jillian had expected. In a slightly faded flannel shirt and jeans, the pastor welcomed them into the small cottage next to the church. He lived alone since the passing of his wife nearly a dozen years before, but the house was very clean, if a bit crowded with dark antique furniture. They sat in front of a small fireplace in the living room. A fire crackled, giving the room a cozy feel, though Jillian noticed the windows were open, probably to keep the room from getting too hot. Early December in Georgia wasn't exactly fireplace weather.

The pastor managed to get the story out of Sidney with barely a sniffle from the teenager. Jillian liked to think it was because she'd already helped the girl release a lot of the pent-up emotion.

"One thing we definitely need to do is let people know these notes are harmless," Jillian said. "I've been trying to figure out what caused the fire at the Clip & Curl. I'm not sure it was an accident. There's some evidence that someone was in the building who shouldn't have been, and that it might have been related to the notes."

"I knew it," Sidney wailed. "I *am* responsible." She immediately burst into tears.

Jillian sighed. *Okay, maybe I'm not very good with this kind of thing.* "I wasn't blaming you," she said.

Keith took the girl's hand. "You are not responsible. If someone started the fire, that is the only person who is responsible. You were trying to prove that ours is a kind and supportive community. I believe that we try to be, but you revealed that we have some growing to do."

Sidney sniffled. "Are you going to tell my parents?"

"I'm not," Pastor Keith said. "But you should. I will not share your identity with anyone. But that doesn't mean someone couldn't find out. Your parents need to know so they have the best chance to keep you safe."

She didn't look happy at the idea, but she reluctantly agreed to tell her parents as soon as she got home.

"And what do you think we should do about telling the community?" Jillian asked.

Pastor Keith held up his hand. "Leave that to me. I'll call the newspaper as soon as you all leave. I think I can ensure a story about the notes that proves their innocent origins without giving out too much information. Sidney, will that be all right with you?"

She nodded eagerly. "Thank you. I didn't know what to do."

Celia had kept surprisingly quiet so far, and Pastor Keith commended her on being a good friend. Celia ducked her head, unusually shy at the compliment from the well-liked pastor. She shrugged. "I knew Jillian would figure out what we should do. That's what she's good at."

"Advice?" Jillian said.

"Figuring things out."

"You *are* good at that," Pastor Keith agreed. "Even if you do act a little rashly at times." He blew out a long breath. "It'll be good to get everyone settled down. This has been a very difficult few days."

"Do you think things will calm down?" Jillian hoped that wasn't overly optimistic. Her experience with Moss Hollow was that folks got ruffled easily and smoothing feathers took considerably longer. Fortunately, the pastor had a lot more experience with feather smoothing than she did.

"I'm sure it will."

After the plans were settled, Jillian led the girls out so Pastor Keith could call the paper. "Why don't you both call your folks," Jillian said. "I'll take you out to supper. You can pick the spot. We could all use something to eat."

Their parents gave permission easily enough, and Jillian followed Sidney's battered yellow VW Bug over to Cheap, Cheap Chicken. It was clear from the amount of chicken both girls ate that their conversation with Pastor Keith had left them feeling much better.

"I've been sick to my stomach all day," Sidney said as she munched on a french fry. "I couldn't even touch my lunch and we were having pizza at school. I love pizza, but just looking at it made me feel like I was going to hurl. I barely ate one of your aunt's cookies."

Celia giggled. "That's because you ate two."

"Oh, you're one to talk," Sidney said. "I saw you shoveling them in. And I was sick earlier."

"I'm sorry to hear you've been so upset," Jillian said quietly.

"She's not lying about being sick at lunch," Celia said. "She was totally green. I could hardly eat my slice from thinking how it made her feel."

Jillian wrinkled her nose, wishing the talk of upset stomachs would end since it was making hers feel a little rocky. "I'm certainly glad you're both feeling better."

"*So* much better," they said in unison, then exchanged glances and giggled.

Jillian wished she shared their relief. On one hand, she was glad to know the notes were benign, but that didn't do anything to explain the salon fire or Poppy's collapse. Of course, Poppy's condition might have nothing to do with the pile of garden fairies in her yard. But maybe it did. The debate continued to rage in Jillian's head well after she'd bid the girls good night and began the drive back to Belle Haven.

Not far from Cheap, Cheap Chicken, she saw the bright lights of Splish Splash and noticed the parking lot was empty. On impulse, Jillian pulled into a parking space near the door. The coin laundry was in a long, squat building with huge glass windows and faux brick trim. The windows presently featured large window clings of happy snowmen and sparkling snowflakes. Jillian knew the decor inside was considerably less cheery, with worn brown carpet and lots of cheap paneling. Bonnie Steck wasn't one to waste money on unnecessary gloss, though she prided herself on her upkeep of the washers and dryers themselves. No one ever lost money or had laundry ruined in one of her machines.

As she sat in the car, Jillian drummed her hands against the top of the steering wheel. *Is this really a good idea?* She could just go home and trust that the newspaper story would settle everyone's mind. After all, the community trusted the pastor. But Jillian wanted to be sure. If she told Bonnie that the notes were benign without revealing anything about the girls, she might be able to jump-start the news that no one needed to worry about them after all. If anyone could get the word around, it would be the person who had spurred on the panic in the community in the first place. *But will Bonnie cooperate?* Jillian certainly knew she was stubborn.

Jillian thought again of how proud Bonnie was that all her machines worked and that she gave patrons a fair return on their money. It was a well-known fact that Bonnie was a stickler for fairness. That thought finally drove her out of the car. She strode quickly to the door, both to get it over with before she thought better of the idea, and because the night was becoming decidedly colder. She was surprised to see the door propped open a crack. *Bonnie must be freezing in there.*

That's when Jillian got close enough to really see the base of the coin laundry door. The thing propping the door open was a hand. Bonnie Steck's hand.

Jillian sat on one of the threadbare plaid sofas and watched the stretcher carrying Bonnie roll through the glass doors and into the night. She wrapped her arms around her middle against the icy chill that seemed to come from inside rather than from the night air.

"Jillian?"

She raised her head, surprised by the almost gentle tone coming from Deputy Gooder Jones. She was used to Gooder being sarcastic, annoyed or scornful, but the effort he was making to be kind made her eyes sting with the tears she had told herself would not fall. "Yes?"

"Why did you come by the coin laundry?" Gooder asked. "Is your washer broken at Belle Haven?"

"No. I wanted to talk to Bonnie about the notes going around town. You know about them?"

Gooder nodded. "She was holding one."

Jillian gaped at him. She hadn't noticed. Of course, she'd mostly been distracted by the blood. *Head wounds bleed a lot*, she reminded herself. *That doesn't mean Bonnie is going to die.* Then the actual words Gooder had just said sank through the fog in her brain. "A new note? That's not possible."

Gooder shrugged. "I don't know if it's new or old. I just know she was holding it. The note has poetry written on it."

"May I see it?"

Gooder frowned. "I haven't bagged it yet." He reached into his jacket and handed Jillian a pair of plastic gloves. She pulled them on, wincing at the sound. Suddenly everything seemed too loud, too rough. Jillian wondered if she'd had one too many shocks. Then Gooder held out a wrinkled piece of paper and Jillian shook off the distracting thoughts and took the paper.

As before, the note was written in careful block letters. Jillian wished she had one of the other notes to compare it to, especially since something about the paper was different, not like the paper she'd seen in the bakery's note. She read the lines aloud. "'One began to weave a crown of tendrils, leaves, and rough nuts brown.'" She flipped the paper over. The back was blank. "This isn't the note she had before."

"How do you know?"

"She was complaining about the other note when she was in the bakery. She said the note compared her face to a cat. There's nothing like that here." She handed it back to Gooder. "But it flatly *cannot* be a new note. At least not from the same person. Maybe she got it from one of the other business owners."

Gooder's expression darkened to suspicion. "And why couldn't it be a new note? Do you know something you need to share with me?"

Jillian blinked against a wash of exhaustion. She felt a pang of guilt for what she was about to do, but she did it anyway. "You need to talk to Pastor Keith."

"Pastor Keith?" Now Gooder's tone changed to something Jillian was more familiar with: suspicion. "Why should I talk to your pastor?"

Jillian folded her arms over her chest. "He's your pastor too, Gooder Jones. And I recommend you not take a tone like that with Pastor Keith. If your grandmother hears of you bullying a pastor, she's going to box your ears."

Gooder actually shuddered. Jillian didn't blame him. Gooder's grandmother made Bertie seem like a cream puff. "Fine. Why should I talk to *our* pastor?"

"I talked to him earlier today, and he knows what's behind the notes. Last I heard, he was going to talk to the newspapers about it to try and restore some sanity to this town. That's why I stopped by here. I wanted to tell Bonnie about it, so she could help calm people down, since she'd certainly helped stir them up."

Gooder didn't answer that for a minute. He stared down at the note in his hands, but Jillian doubted he was really seeing it. "You think someone got a little too stirred up?"

Jillian shrugged. "I think the fire at the salon wasn't an accident. And I think it was tied to the notes."

"Why? Was someone at the salon involved with the note writing?"

Jillian shook her head. "You're really behind the gossip here, Gooder. Bonnie accused Bertie and Cornelia of being the reason for the notes." She tapped the note in his hands. "Are you familiar with that poem?"

"Not really. I knew about the poems, of course. Everyone in Moss Hollow heard about the poems. The sheriff's department got over a dozen calls about it. I heard it was something about goblins. As we told all those callers, this isn't a sheriff's department matter—well, not until now."

"The poem is a kind of fairy tale about a girl who is bewitched by goblins. She's saved from going mad by her brave sister. Bonnie decided that was the story of Bertie and Cornelia's life." She rolled her eyes at the idea.

"And she said this to Bertie?" Gooder asked.

"She did."

"Maybe I should be asking Bertie where she was this evening," Gooder said.

Jillian glared at him. "That is not funny. And she's been at Belle Haven all evening. You can ask Cornelia." Jillian realized she hadn't actually *seen* her grandmother at Belle Haven, but Cornelia had mentioned going to ask Bertie what she wanted for supper, so obviously Cornelia knew Bertie was there. Besides, accusing Bertie was ridiculous.

"I will," Gooder said, then held up a hand before Jillian could blast him. "Not because I think she bashed Bonnie in the head. But if they had a public altercation, I have to follow up."

"Terrific, but the *conversation* between Bonnie and Bertie ended up with Bonnie pursuing a new theory. She decided the poem was about Jasmine and Poppy instead because Poppy was wild about fairies."

"I don't like the sound of this."

"Jasmine and Bonnie also had a *public altercation*, until Pastor Keith came up and put a stop to the yelling in front of the church. Then within a few hours, the salon burned down, and Poppy ended up in the hospital."

"You think someone attacked Poppy?" Gooder was visibly shocked. "Why is this the first I've heard of it?"

Jillian ignored the second question and answered the first, "I think someone went to her house and pulled all the fairies out of her flower beds. And I think someone left Jasmine a note on one of the whiteboards at the salon. A note ending with 'or else.'"

"Or else what?"

"I couldn't tell. The whiteboard had clearly been blasted by a fire hose. The 'or else' was saved because the board fell behind something." Jillian fished her phone out of her jacket pocket and found the photo. She handed the phone to Gooder.

"Why were you poking around the salon?" Gooder asked as he poked at the screen, enlarging the photo.

"Jasmine asked me to. She felt like there was more going on than an accidental fire. And she's certain no one at the salon left a curling iron plugged in."

"No one thinks they make mistakes like that," Gooder said.

"But the fire marshal is absolutely certain. The fire was caused when a curling iron fell into a wastepaper basket. And the curling iron was plugged in. Since it obviously didn't happen with anyone there, the only possible answer is that someone left it plugged in."

"Or someone plugged it back in," Jillian said quietly.

Jillian could practically watch the wheels spinning in Gooder's head, but what he came out with made her feel like smacking him. "Maybe Jasmine plugged it in and dropped it in the basket. The insurance company suggested that might be the case."

"The insurance company doesn't know Jasmine and how much she loves that shop." She followed her impulse and smacked Gooder in the arm. "You do. Now think like someone with good sense. The someone who plugged in the curling iron also left the threatening note."

Gooder rubbed his arm. "You know, you're getting more like your grandmother every day. Why threaten someone and then burn the place down? You don't need the threat if you're going to go ahead and do it."

"Unless they were threatening something even worse." Jillian finally let her eyes drift to the bloodstained carpet. She winced at the sight. "And something much worse definitely happened."

Even Gooder couldn't argue with that.

By the time Jillian got home, her aunt and grandmother had both retired for the night. Jillian doubted they were asleep, and she considered knocking on Bertie's door for a chat. She even went so far as to stand outside the door to Bertie's downstairs suite, but suddenly the thought of talking about Bonnie was too much. She went upstairs instead.

At the top of the stairs, Possum sat with his tail wrapped neatly around him, delicately washing his face.

"You're looking suspiciously innocent," she told him.

Possum blinked in the long, slow way of cats that hinted at secrets kept, though Jillian knew Possum well enough to know the most exciting secret the cat harbored was his addiction to eating bugs. She reached down and gently scratched between his ears. "I had a long day, buddy. So don't wander around yowling later, okay?"

Possum bumped her hand with his head and Jillian gave him a soft pat before walking on to her room. She had just opened the door when she heard another door open nearby.

Cornelia called to her in a loud whisper, "Jillian! Come and see this."

Jillian turned to give her aunt a tired smile. She didn't have the energy to resist, though she considered it when she walked into Cornelia's room to find magazine subscription tear-out cards strewn across her bed. "It's late," Jillian said. "Could we do paper crafts tomorrow?"

"Don't be sassy," Cornelia said. "Earlier I was trying to get a sense of what secrets you are keeping with the girls."

"It would be better if you forgot all about their visit," Jillian said.

Cornelia waved that away. "I didn't get anything sensible, but Possum grabbed one of the cards and ran out into the hall with it. The rascal hid under the highboy and had the card half chewed up before I could get it away from him."

"That explains his exile to the hallway," Jillian said. "I thought it was suspicious."

"Never mind that. I just realized why he ran off with the card."

"Because you handle the tear-out cards while eating snacks, and they smell like food?" Jillian suggested.

Her aunt gave her a scornful frown. "It was because Raymond wanted to give me a message."

Where did I make the wrong turn with my life? Jillian wondered. She loved her aunt dearly, but Cornelia could be more than a little flaky and the most obvious sign was her unshakable belief that her late husband somehow kept in contact with her through the cat. Jillian had never seen any sign of Uncle Raymond in Possum beyond the cat's clear affection for Cornelia. But Cornelia also snuck the tubby cat bacon behind Bertie's back, so Jillian was fairly certain the affection was bought and paid for.

"Don't give me that face," Cornelia snapped. "Look at this." She thrust a half-chewed and still slightly soggy scrap of paper at her.

With a wince, Jillian took the paper, trying not to touch the soggy parts.

The scrap of cardstock was the subscription card from a mystery magazine. "I didn't know the salon subscribed to any mystery magazines," she said. She knew Cornelia had gotten most of her tear-out cards from the old magazines at the Clip & Curl.

"They don't," Cornelia said. "Josi gave me some cards."

"Josi! You've roped Josi into this? Don't let Bertie know. She'll yell at her for encouraging you, and I don't think Josi could take the strain."

Cornelia sniffed. "I'm hardly likely to discuss my forays into the spirit realm with Bertie. She has no imagination at all. It's hard to believe we're genetically linked."

"I think I've heard Bertie say something similar." Jillian held up the tattered paper. "What am I supposed to be gleaning from this?"

"Isn't it obvious?" Cornelia snatched the card from her and tapped the tiny magazine cover printed on the paper. "Read the title of the cover story: 'Beware the Herring.' It's talking about this business with the weird poetry notes. I'm sure of it. Raymond thinks we should look deeper into the clues. We're being distracted from the truth somehow."

"*We?*"

"Fine, *you*," Cornelia snapped. "I know Jasmine asked you to investigate the fire and the vandalism at Poppy's house. You need to be careful not to be drawn off by a red herring."

"I haven't found any fish," Jillian said sarcastically. She refused to go along with any of this foolishness. She couldn't get her aunt to stop using her tear-out cards, but Jillian certainly didn't have to support it. "But I have had a long day, and I need to go to bed."

Cornelia glared at her. "You're intentionally being obtuse. You know what a red herring is in a mystery. It's something that seems important at the time, but isn't in the long run."

"Fine. I'll keep your theory in mind."

"Good. Now tell me what's going on with those girls."

"No. I believe I've already told you it's not my story to tell." Jillian pointed at her aunt. "And I'm not kidding. You need to forget you saw them here tonight. And don't tell *anyone* about it. Does Bertie know they were here?"

Cornelia shook her head. "She came out of her room long enough to get a pitifully small sandwich, then headed back in. She said she had to go over the books for the bakery. We really need to make more of an effort to eat together. It's an important part of staying strong as a family."

Jillian knew Cornelia hated to eat alone. She gave Cornelia's hand a gentle squeeze. "Sorry I left you to have supper alone. I'll try harder." She suddenly felt an overwhelming urge to unburden herself. "After I left the girls, I went by Splish Splash."

Cornelia pursed her lips. "I hope you didn't sit on any of the furniture. I am not completely comfortable with Bonnie Steck's views on cleanliness."

"Bonnie is in the hospital. She was assaulted."

Cornelia gasped and paled slightly.

"Aunt Cornelia, are you all right?" Jillian asked.

"That was the other article on this card." She held up the battered paper. "'Assault and Battery 101.'"

"Aunt Cornelia, that doesn't mean anything. It's a mystery magazine. Probably half the articles have to do with assault. It's a coincidence."

Cornelia shook her head. "It's a sign." She reached out and grabbed Jillian's hand. "You have to be careful. Beware the herring."

"Fine, I will. I promise."

Jillian spent a few more minutes with her aunt until she was sure Cornelia was okay. Then she finally made it to her room. It was still a little early to go to bed, even with the early hours they kept at the bakery. Jillian considered settling down with a book, but she decided on a soothing bath instead.

She glanced at the small tub in her bathroom. Down the hall was a bathroom with a huge claw-foot tub that was perfect for soaking. Jillian decided that was exactly what she needed after the difficult night she'd had. She slipped out of her clothes and pulled on a thick robe, but when she searched for her slippers, she only found one. "Possum strikes again."

She opened the bedroom door and peered up and down the hall but saw no sign of her slipper. Refusing to let that stop her plan for a soothing bath, she headed to the bathroom, her gait slightly uneven from only wearing one slipper.

In the big bathroom, the tiles felt shockingly cold on her bare foot and she hurried over to the fluffy bath mat and filled the tub. She sank into the hot water with a deeply satisfied sigh. She'd been right. *This is what I needed.*

The warmth of the water unraveled the knots in her back and soothed away the tension of the day. Jillian let idle thoughts slip through her head, not even trying to wrangle them into any orderly processing of what she'd experienced. She'd do that tomorrow. For now, she was focused on relaxing.

The hot soak had almost lulled her to sleep when there was a sharp rap on the door. She jumped in surprise, sloshing a spray of water over the side of the tub.

"I'll be out in a minute!" she called.

Her aunt's voice was muffled through the door. "This is important."

Sadly, Jillian climbed out. She grabbed her robe with wrinkly fingers and wrapped it around herself. "Come in."

The door opened and Aunt Cornelia poked her head in. "Sorry to bother you, dear. I heard your cell phone ringing. I knew you might not want to miss a call so I answered it."

Jillian wasn't sure she liked the idea of Cornelia answering her phone, but she knew her aunt meant well, and something about Cornelia's expression killed her urge to scold the older woman. "Yes?"

"It was Gooder," Cornelia said. "He said he thought you ought to know."

"Know what?"

"Bonnie Steck didn't make it. She's dead. Someone has murdered her."

After a night of unpleasant dreams and worry, the alarm clock seemed particularly malicious as it cut through Jillian's sleep like a razor. She slapped at it and accidentally sent it tumbling to the floor where it continued to shriek, forcing her to get up to quiet it.

Her room was completely dark. One of the things she liked least about the coming winter was the shortening of the daylight hours, which meant she got up long before her brain considered it morning. She wondered if she should get a timer to switch on a light along with the alarm in the morning. It might feel more like morning if there was light.

Shuffling through her morning routine seemed to take extra time, and Jillian realized she was intentionally clinging to a sleepy fog to avoid the thoughts that lurked just beyond it. Images of Bonnie's hand, caught in the door of the coin laundry. The sound of her aunt's voice as she related the news of Bonnie's death. Jillian didn't know any possible way she could have prevented anything that had happened in the last week, but she felt guilty about it anyway.

After splashing water in her face, she stared into her eyes in the mirror. "Stop thinking like that. It won't help. The answers are out there."

The face that stared back at her didn't seem convinced. Jillian gave up on the argument and focused on getting ready for work. She had no doubt that the bakery would be buzzing with the latest news all day.

When she finally got downstairs, the smell of coffee did as much to wake her up as the water splashed in her face. She headed straight for the pot in the kitchen.

"Pastor Keith's revelation made the papers," Cornelia said. "Everyone is going to be wondering who he's covering for."

Jillian faced her aunt and grandmother, cradling the mug of coffee. "Not every question needs an answer."

"That's a new viewpoint, coming from you." Bertie tapped the folded newspaper that lay in the middle of the breakfast table. "Clearly Cornelia knows to whom the article refers. She's practically humming with the secret."

Jillian studied her aunt. Realistically, she'd known her aunt would make the connection between the teenagers and the pastor, but she'd harbored false hope. Cornelia wasn't exactly known for her ability to keep things to herself. "You know you cannot tell anyone."

Cornelia mimed locking her lips with an invisible key and throwing it away. Oddly, Jillian didn't feel reassured.

"She's so annoying when she has a secret," Bertie grumbled. "And if she knows, why don't I? I live here too."

Jillian shuffled over to sit with them and took the top piece of toast from a plate piled high. "I certainly didn't *tell* Aunt Cornelia. It was a case of being in the wrong place at the right time."

Her grandmother picked up a slice of toast and began buttering it vigorously. "Well, I hope you and Pastor Keith have a plan for when it gets out, because it will. Your aunt flatly cannot keep a secret."

"I can too," Cornelia snapped. "I've never told anyone that we dye our hair, for instance."

Bertie rolled her eyes. "We're over eighty years old and still blonde. Everyone knows we dye our hair."

Cornelia sniffed. "Maybe, but *I* didn't tell them."

Bertie tore her toast in two and glanced sharply at Jillian. "How are you doing? The paper also had a story about Bonnie. Cornelia said you found her."

Jillian shuddered. "I did, but I didn't know she was dying."

Her grandmother shook her head slowly. "What's our town coming to? This isn't New York or even Atlanta. No one expects a mugging in Moss Hollow."

Jillian stopped absently tearing off bits of her toast. "You think it was a mugging?"

"That article certainly hinted at it."

Jillian glanced toward the folded newspaper and wondered if she should read the account, but the thought of going through it again depressed her. "She was clutching a note—one like the others with poetry copied on it."

Bertie's eyes widened. "*That* wasn't in the article."

Cornelia harrumphed. "Gooder was probably trying to be all big city."

Jillian had no idea what her aunt meant. "What?"

"Like on television crime shows. They hold back clues so that if someone gives a false confession, they'll be able to tell."

"Since when do you watch crime shows?" Jillian rarely saw either her aunt or grandmother watch television. She knew Bertie had a TV in the sitting room of her suite, but Jillian thought books were more their entertainment of choice.

"I have a television in my craft room," Cornelia said. "Sometimes I enjoy listening to something while I'm doing handwork. Plus, I thought I might learn some pointers from the shows. Considering how often this family finds itself caught up in one mystery or another, I think we could all use some insight."

"From television?" Jillian said dryly.

"You can learn a lot from television," Cornelia said. Then she gazed at Bertie. "And I don't know why you're picking on me, sister. At least I don't watch reality TV competitions like some people I could name."

Jillian gazed at her grandmother. The older woman's cheeks reddened and she refused to meet Jillian's eyes. "Only the cooking shows."

"Bertie Alfreda, I've *seen* you watching one of those shows where they cart people out to an island and make them act like fools for money."

Bertie glared at her. "I was just flipping through the channels. And I'll ask you not to barge into my suite without knocking." Bertie dusted toast crumbs off her hands. "I have no idea why we're wasting time talking rubbish. I need to get to work."

Jillian watched her grandmother storm away from the table. *You never know what's going on with people.* That thought brought her back to Bonnie's attack. Someone in Moss Hollow had a much bigger secret than bad TV. And Jillian suspected that someone better figure out what was going on before more people were hurt.

As she'd expected, the bakery was a madhouse, but Jillian finally had a tiny bit of good news. Maggie was well enough to work, so she could deal with the long line of gossipy customers while Jillian threw herself into tackling the list of orders.

To Jillian's surprise, the bakery had been open about an hour when Savannah came in through the back entrance, tying an apron around herself as she walked. Bertie caught sight of her and smacked herself lightly in the forehead, leaving a flour-covered partial handprint there. "I forgot to call you," Bertie said. "I'm so sorry. I asked you to come in because we were getting behind with Jillian working the front counter, but I should have let you know that Maggie came in today."

"I can still help if you want," Savannah said. "I have the day off. And like my grandmother always said, many hands make light work."

"In that case, I'd love it if you'd help Jillian with the cookie orders. I think every teacher in Moss Hollow decided to have early holiday parties this year."

Savannah snatched a hairnet from the box. "Great. I love making cookies."

"You're a darlin'," Bertie said. "And this way I can send Lenora to the wholesaler in Painter's Ridge. I didn't order enough pecans, and we're going to run out."

"I'm happy to go," Lenora said cheerfully. "I wanted to run by the handcraft store they have there in the old post office building. I saw the cutest wooden popgun that I wanted to get for Henry."

Jillian stared at Lenora in surprise. She knew Lenora loved buying presents for her "grandbaby," but she was surprised his mother, Dorie, let him have guns and said as much.

Lenora flapped a hand at that. "A popgun isn't a gun. It's just a noisemaker. Besides, I had a cap gun when I was a little girl. I thought I was Annie Oakley. It didn't hurt me none, and a popgun won't hurt that boy. Young parents today want to wrap kids in cotton and set them on a shelf. That's no way to grow up."

Jillian almost laughed. She suspected she was hearing one of the reasons why Lenora and her daughter squabbled a fair bit.

As Bertie added to the errands for Lenora to run in Painter's Ridge, Jillian and Savannah began gathering ingredients for the cookie orders. But they could still hear the conversation between Lenora and Bertie.

"If you don't mind," Lenora said. "I'll stop in and check on Poppy when I'm done with this."

"Of course," Bertie agreed as she finished scribbling the list.

"How is Poppy doing?" Savannah asked.

Lenora's cheerful smile slipped away. "The same. But she's not worse, so I'm not about to give up hope."

"Good for you," Savannah said. "She's in my prayers."

"I do appreciate that," Lenora said. Then she took the list from Bertie and headed out the back door of the bakery.

Since most of their ingredients and mixers were in the same area, Jillian and Savannah worked on their cookies side by side.

Savannah broke eggs into her mixing bowl. "I heard about Bonnie. It must have been horrible for you."

"You knew I was there?" Jillian said. "I heard my name wasn't in the paper."

"James told me."

"How did he hear it?"

Savannah raised a shoulder. "If I had to guess, I'd say the leak was Gooder's mom. I'm sure you're aware that she works part-time as a dispatcher at the sheriff's office."

Jillian nodded. Gooder's mother had answered her emergency calls more than once. "Why would she tell James?"

Savannah cracked another egg. "She didn't. She told April Meyer. April is Mrs. Jones's best friend. And she must be about the biggest gossip in Moss Hollow, possibly excluding the Sweetie Pies. Anyway, April told Patsy down at the post office, and Patsy told James when he went in to get his mail from the post office box this morning."

"I didn't think the post office was open this early," Jillian said.

Savannah wiped her fingers on her apron and picked up another egg. "It's not, but the public access to post office boxes is. And Patsy *just happened* to be sweeping the floor around the post office boxes, even though that isn't her job. James said she pounced on him like a chicken on a June bug. He figured she was just waiting for someone to gossip with. A juicy secret is like that. It just wants to get out."

Jillian managed a slight smile. "Poor James." Then she sighed. "And poor Bonnie."

Savannah nodded. "Bonnie wasn't the easiest person to deal with. But it's just horrible what happened to her."

Jillian scooped brown sugar into the mixer with a slightly shaky hand. "I can't get the image of her lying in the doorway out of my head." She set the measuring cup down. "She was holding a note."

Savannah stopped breaking eggs to gape at Jillian. "Patsy didn't know that part. Did you see what it said?"

"It was another quote from 'Goblin Market.'"

Savannah sucked in a sharp breath. "Do you think the note writer attacked Bonnie? I read the piece about the notes in today's paper. Pastor Keith made the note writer sound harmless."

"The note writer *is* harmless," Jillian insisted. "This note was different. The more I think about it, the more different it becomes. The paper was different somehow, and there was nothing written on the back."

"I wonder if any of the other notes were blank on the back."

Jillian shrugged. "I haven't talked to everyone who got one. But I'm beginning to think I should, or at least I should talk to the people who went to the council meeting. I'm sure there were people who got notes and didn't attend."

Savannah picked up the last egg from the bowl and gave it a sharp tap on the table. "Well, if you want me to come with you, just let me know." She dumped the egg into the bowl. "You know, you could put the Sweetie Pies on the task of calling all the shop owners. I don't know about the others, but I'm sure Maudie and Wanda Jean would love it. They live for all that sleuthing stuff."

"I don't know if I'm ready to pull Maudie and Wanda Jean into this," Jillian said. "Anything they learned would immediately be dumped into the gossip network."

Before Savannah could respond, Maggie popped her head in the doorway. "Deputy Jones is here. He wants to talk to someone in charge."

"Send him back here," Bertie called from her spot at the big mixers. "I'd just as soon not chat with a deputy in the customer area."

"Will do!" Maggie sang out.

She disappeared back through the doorway and within moments, Gooder walked into the kitchen. He stared around curiously. "You know, I don't think I've been back here since my elementary school class took a tour."

Bertie walked over, wiping her hands on her apron. "As I recall, you got in trouble for climbing into my big mixing bowl."

"It was a dare," Gooder said. He jerked a thumb at Jillian. "From her."

"I don't remember that at all," Jillian lied with a sweet smile.

"Can I help you, Deputy?" Bertie asked. "Or do you want to see if you still fit in the big bowl?"

Gooder grinned. "I have grown up since then. I'm collecting the notes from all the business owners, at least all the owners who kept them. Do you still have yours?"

Bertie nodded. "Wait here." She walked through the doorway to the front of the bakery.

Gooder wandered over to stand near Jillian and Savannah. He gazed with interest at what Jillian was doing. "Chocolate chip cookies?"

"Yup. And don't stick your finger in the batter. There are health codes for things like that."

"I won't," Gooder protested. "Like I told your grandmother, I've grown up. But I wouldn't say no to some chocolate chips." He offered her a smile.

Jillian rolled her eyes and picked up the bowl she'd filled with chips. She tipped a few into Gooder's hand. "So, how many notes have you collected so far?"

"Three. You'd be surprised how few people kept theirs."

"Are they first or second notes? Can you tell? I'd like to know if the first notes are the same as the one Bonnie was holding." Jillian asked.

"All three are written in block letters," Gooder said. He peered over the edge of Savannah's mixing bowl. "What kind of cookies are you making?"

"Sugar," Savannah said, waving a rubber spatula at him. "No chips from me."

"Do you have any leads other than the note she was holding?" Jillian asked. "Because I can tell you right now that the person who wrote all the notes for the businesses did not attack Bonnie."

Gooder gave her a narrow-eyed stare. "So you say."

Jillian abandoned all semblance of working on the cookies and gave Gooder her full attention. "So Pastor Keith says. Did you talk to him?"

"I did. And I value his insight, but I'd value it a lot more if he'd tell me who the culprit was. He's says he can't breech the person's confidentiality."

Jillian huffed. "Well, I trust him."

"That nice," Gooder snapped, "but you're not in law enforcement. You just think you are."

Jillian poked him in the chest and he took a step back. "You need to investigate somewhere else," she said. "This may be tied to the notes, but it's not tied to the note writer, not the original one anyway. But there have been a lot of people worked up over them, including Bonnie. She was leading the charge on Sunday."

"I've heard."

"So maybe someone she accused didn't appreciate it. Just at the church she attacked my grandmother *and* Jasmine. I'm inclined to wonder who else she went after. She was digging at people. And folks don't like that."

"You should know," Gooder growled.

"Right!" Jillian said, smacking the table for emphasis. "How many times have people gone after me for asking a few innocent questions? And Bonnie wasn't doing it nearly as sweetly as I do."

Gooder barked out a laugh at Jillian's characterization of herself as sweet.

"What is going on back here?" Bertie demanded as she stormed back in carrying the note. "It took me forever to find this. Apparently someone used it for a coaster." She gave Jillian the stink eye, but Jillian held up her hands in protest. Bertie held the note out to Gooder.

"You compare that to the note Bonnie had," Jillian said, tapping the paper as Gooder took it. "You'll see they're not by the same person. Then you can look into who might have been mad at Bonnie."

"You were kind enough to tell me two suspects," Gooder said as he slipped the note into a clear sleeve. "Jasmine and your grandmother."

"You listen up," Bertie snapped. "Jasmine has suffered enough. Her sister is very ill. Her hands are burned. Her business is closed. She doesn't need grief from you."

"Yes, she's had some terrible things happen. Which leads me to an interesting question. Does she blame Bonnie for what happened? And did she do something about it?"

Jillian didn't know what to say to that. She'd actually provided Jasmine with some reason to blame someone for the fire, someone who had written an ultimatum on the whiteboard and then had set her shop on fire. And the first person Jasmine had suspected was Bonnie. She'd said as much right in front of Jillian and Savannah.

"I'm not sure Jasmine *could* assault anyone," Savannah said. "When Jillian and I were out to her house, she couldn't even open a jar of pickles. I couldn't see her overpowering someone as tough as Bonnie."

"You'd be surprised what rage can do for a person," Gooder informed her.

"Clearly there's no talking to you, Gooder Jones, so get out of my bakery and go investigate," Bertie said, her voice full of the same exasperation that showed on her face. "Go bother the poor woman. Just go. I have work to do here. You best hope I don't report you to the sheriff."

"Or Lenora," Jillian added.

Eyes wide at that prospect, Gooder went. Bertie grumpily resumed work on her bread dough.

With a sigh, Jillian turned back to the recipe. *How much brown sugar did I put in?*

"What do you think?" Savannah asked.

"About what?"

"About Jasmine. As they say in the mysteries, she has motive. Do you think she could have hurt Bonnie?"

Jillian shook her head. "Of course not." She scooped up another cup of sugar and dumped it in her bowl. "Probably not."

"Probably not," Savannah agreed.

Jillian set the mixer whirring and stared at the paddle. *I hope not. I truly do.*

10

By late afternoon, the question of Jasmine's involvement was stuck in Jillian's head like a bad tune. As she carefully piped frosting onto the sugar cookies Savannah had made, she could think of nothing else. Jasmine believed someone had burned down her salon and someone had been in Poppy's garden, which meant someone also might have been involved with Poppy's condition. Jasmine had been certain that the "someone" in both cases was Bonnie.

"I'm going to have to talk to her," Jillian finally said.

Savannah was gently folding egg whites into a cake batter. "Who?"

Jillian sat her pastry bag down and spoke in a whisper. "Jasmine. She had cause to attack Bonnie. I need to know if she had opportunity. I want to hear it from her."

"She lives alone," Savannah said. "I doubt she has an alibi."

"She doesn't need one," Jillian said. "Not for me anyway. I just want to talk to her and see her face so I can put this idea to rest in my own head."

"What you two whispering about?" Lenora asked as she walked into the kitchen, loaded with bags from her errands. She frowned at the scant number of cookies Jillian had finished decorating. "I hope you have a whole lot of decorated cookies hiding somewhere, or your grandma is going to skin your hide for talking instead of working."

"Bertie has never had a problem with talking," Jillian said as Lenora began unloading the bags she'd brought in.

"Still," Savannah said as she scraped her batter into cake pans. "We're starting to talk in circles, and I need to run to an appointment. Since Lenora is back, is it all right if I go? I can put the timer on so someone can pull these cakes when they're done."

"No problem," Lenora said.

"We're just grateful for your help," Jillian said. "You've been a lifesaver."

"That's me, a lifesaver." She grinned, showing off a dimple in her cheek. "I'm going to have dinner with James tonight. But call if you need anything."

"You two just have fun," Jillian said.

As soon as Savannah left, Jillian got back to work on the cookies. She had to admit, Lenora had a point. She should have been done by now. "At least this is the last pan of cookies to decorate." She picked up a decorating bag loaded with green buttercream frosting. She carefully piped a holly leaf on the cookie.

Lenora peeked at the finished cookies already on trays and loaded onto one of the rolling carts. Then she grabbed a couple of bags of pecans from the table. "Let me put this in the cooler, and then I'll help with the last of those cookies."

As soon as she came back, Jillian blurted out the question that had been nagging at her. "Lenora, Jasmine is your cousin. Do you think she's capable of violence?"

Lenora picked up a second pastry bag and began decorating one of the blank cookies. "Sugar," she said, "*anyone* is capable of violence with enough cause."

"Jasmine believes someone burned her salon on purpose," Jillian said. "And vandalized Poppy's garden. Which means the person might have hurt Poppy, even indirectly if Poppy was running out to stop them from pulling up her fairies."

"'Believes,'" Lenora said scornfully. "'Might.' Sounds like idle speculation to me."

"Still, if Jasmine believed Bonnie hurt Poppy, would Jasmine have gone after Bonnie?"

Lenora paused and met her eyes. "My family isn't some backwoods clan. If Jasmine believed Bonnie burned her salon or had a hand in Poppy's condition, she would have called the sheriff."

"I still think I need to talk to her," Jillian said. "I need to hear it out of her mouth myself."

"You're likely to hear all kinds of things out of her mouth if you go accusing her of murder," Lenora said.

Jillian suspected Lenora was right, but she still knew she had to talk to Jasmine. Somewhere in all this chaos lay the answer. And Jillian knew she wasn't the only one in Moss Hollow who wouldn't rest easy until that answer was uncovered.

She and Lenora settled into an unusually tense silence as they finished the cookies. Jillian set the last cookie on the tray just as Maggie poked her head around the kitchen door. "Jillian, you've got company."

Jillian wheeled the full cart toward the doorway. "Gooder again?"

"Nope, but it *is* a guy," Maggie said with a mischievous grin. "A hunky guy."

That made Jillian laugh. "No one says hunky anymore."

"I do." Maggie gestured to the cart of filled trays. "Do I put all that in the front cases? Because I don't think I have that much room."

Jillian shook her head. "No, I just need to park this as far from the steamier parts of the kitchen as I can so the frosting will set. Then we need to box them for the elementary school."

Maggie bobbed her head and disappeared back through the doorway. Jillian had a fair idea who the "hunky guy" must be, so she pulled off her hairnet and apron before slipping through the doorway.

Hunter stood a short distance from the displays, people-watching out the window. As she studied him, Jillian had to admit that "hunky" wasn't a bad description, even if it wasn't one she would have chosen. Hunter had spent much of his free time during the late summer and fall working on an old house he'd bought. She could see that his suit fit a bit tighter through the shoulders and chest as a result, and he sported a considerably darker tan than morticians ever did on television.

She slid around the counter. "Hi Hunter. What a lovely surprise."

His usual warm smile was missing, his expression one of concern as he took her hand. "I heard about Bonnie. Are you all right?"

Jillian nodded, enjoying the warm feeling of her hand engulfed in his. "Still horrified, but I've been trying not to think too much about the actual experience."

His expression darkened still further. "I hope Deputy Jones wasn't unkind to you."

Jillian nearly laughed at that. "Actually Gooder was unusually sensitive. I almost made him show me his ID. Of course, he's back to normal today." She nodded toward an empty table. "Want to sit? I could use a minute off my feet."

He indicated the line at the counter as they walked to the table. "You do seem busy."

"It's that time of year. We stay swamped from a couple weeks before Thanksgiving, and things don't really die down until after New Year's Day, only to ramp back up for Valentine's Day."

He pulled out a chair for Jillian. "Sounds exhausting."

"Sometimes." Jillian slipped into the chair with a murmur of thanks.

Hunter sat down across the small table and took her hand again. "I assume you aren't going to put all this behind you and refuse to think about it anymore."

"I don't see how I can. Right now, I think Gooder's number one suspect is Jasmine. I promised her that I would check out the fire at her salon. If that led to Bonnie's death, I need to know."

Hunter raised his eyebrows. "*You* suspect Jasmine?"

"Not really." She sighed. "Or at least not much. Did you see the article about the notes in today's paper?"

"I did. I expect Pastor Keith's life is going to be interesting for a while. I'm not sure too many people are ready to let go of the conspiracy theories about the notes."

"They should," Jillian said. "I'm absolutely positive there is no tie between the note writer and the fire or Bonnie's attack."

Once again Hunter's eyebrows went up. "You know who wrote the notes?" Then he gave a rueful smile. "Of course you do."

"I didn't go hunting for that particular revelation," Jillian said. "It came to me. But I do know, and I'm certain that note writer's intentions were harmless."

"The article said the notes were meant to prove the citizens of Moss Hollow wouldn't go on a witch hunt just because of something weird. If that's true, the one thing I know about the person is that he's naive."

Jillian sadly had to agree with that, but before she could speak, a small group of women bustled into the bakery and made a beeline straight for their table. Although most of the women were regulars at the bakery, nothing about their serious expressions boded well for the next few minutes.

Mellie Flanigan reached the table first and stood clutching her purse in front of her like a shield. "You saw Bonnie last night."

"I did."

Mellie narrowed her eyes as the rest of her group crowded in behind her. "Is it true she had one of those horrible notes? Does that mean Pastor Keith is wrong and the notes aren't over?"

"Ladies," Hunter said, as he rose from his seat, "as you can imagine, finding Bonnie after her attack was very traumatic. Jillian doesn't need to relive it."

Mellie aimed her sharp gaze at him. "None of us want this nightmare to go on for one moment more, but it doesn't seem like we have much choice, does it?"

Jillian stood up so she didn't have to look up to the shorter woman. "You were part of Bonnie's paranoid posse at church. When was the last time you saw her?"

Mellie drew back slightly, as if sensing an accusation in Jillian's question. "Sunday. We had brunch together after church at the Southern Peach Inn."

"All of you?" Jillian asked, letting her gaze take in the other three women standing behind Mellie. She recognized two of the women from the group at church, but the third was a complete stranger to her.

"No, just Bonnie and me."

"Because the rest of us weren't invited," Bess Holland snapped, stepping away from the other two slightly.

"You *were* invited," Mellie insisted. "You chose not to come."

Bess sniffed. "I don't remember being invited. I would certainly have gone. I had to go home and watch Joe stare at the TV screen all afternoon while grown men raced around bouncing a ball."

"Well, I didn't want to go," one of the women behind Bess said. "I can make a perfectly nice Sunday dinner without spending all that money."

The last woman in the group who hadn't made a remark up until then snorted. "Please, Norrie, you're so tight I'm surprised you don't squeak when you walk. I'm sure I would have gone if I'd been invited."

"I don't remember anyone being *disinvited*," Mellie said, "but you know how hard it is to get a table at the Southern Peach Inn for Sunday brunch. It is completely impossible with a big group."

"So why you?" Bess snapped. "How did you get to be the big cheese?"

"Ladies," Hunter said gently, "is this the place for an argument?"

Jillian appreciated his attempt to keep conflict out of the bakery, but she did find the dissent interesting. She wondered how much conflict existed in the ranks of Bonnie's group. "Did Bonnie mention being worried about anything other than the notes?" Jillian asked to draw Mellie's attention. "Was there anyone she was having trouble with?"

"I think the notes were more than enough to worry about," Mellie said. "And clearly they still are." She narrowed her eyes at Jillian. "And clearly you know more about them than you're telling. How come you're always in the thick of things, Jillian Green?"

"Just lucky, I suppose. How long did your brunch last?"

"Hours," Mellie said. "We had a lot to discuss."

"Like what?" Bess demanded. The other two women murmured agreement with the question.

Mellie shifted nervously and seemed to clutch her purse even tighter. "We're wandering off purpose here. We demand to know what is going on in Moss Hollow before we all end up murdered in our beds."

"Bonnie wasn't in bed," Bess pointed out.

Mellie shot a glare in her direction, then shifted back to Jillian. "So who is behind those notes?"

"Why ask me?" Jillian asked, genuinely curious. "You're clearly familiar with the newspaper article. Why not ask Pastor Keith?"

"We did," Bess said. "He wouldn't tell us."

"Bess, hush up!" Mellie snapped. "You don't have to tell her our business."

"But I'm supposed to answer your questions?" Jillian asked, keeping her tone mild but folding her arms over her chest.

"We have a right to know!" Mellie punctuated her remark with a stamp of her foot.

"Right here, right now, you have a right to a buy a brownie or cookie or any pastry you like," Jillian said as she sat back down in the bistro chair. "And that's about it." Hunter followed her example and sat down across from her.

Mellie stamped her foot again. "We will not be dismissed."

"You're going to be a lot worse than dismissed!" Bertie's voice boomed from behind the counter. "Y'all need to get in line and make your purchase or march on out of here. You're annoying our real customers and harassing my granddaughter."

Mellie gave Bertie a narrow-eyed glower. "You don't scare me."

Clearly the other two didn't feel the same way. Jillian saw Norrie had slipped away the second Bertie began speaking and ducked into the restroom. The other woman was slowly easing toward the door. Only Mellie and Bess seemed inclined to stand their ground.

"Fine," Bertie said. "But this is still my place of business." She raised her voice slightly. "Maggie, call the sheriff's department. Tell them we have some kind of problem here, and I'd appreciate it if they'd send out a deputy."

Mellie gasped. "You wouldn't dare."

Bess clearly thought Bertie *would* dare. She whirled and headed toward the exit. Mellie realized she had no backing left. "Bess, where are you going?"

"I just remembered I'm scheduled to help out at the kids' school today." She darted through the door.

"You still want to chat with the deputies?" Bertie asked Mellie.

Mellie's bravado collapsed, and she harrumphed once before following Bess out the door.

"Sorry for the disruption," Bertie said to the other patrons. "Maggie will be happy to help you with your purchases now."

From his place in line, Gordon Sprague applauded. "That was a fine job of intimidation, Bertie. You nearly scared me."

Bertie gave him a fierce frown, and he grinned and focused on the pastry displays. The line at the counter became very tidy as Bertie marched back to the kitchen.

"Well, that was very dramatic," Hunter said. "Do you often have so much drama here?"

"More often than I prefer," Jillian said with a sigh.

Hunter chuckled. "I'm not sure I completely believe that. But I need to head out myself. Can I talk you into dinner tomorrow night? I would ask you to join me tonight too, but I am afraid I have some work to do, given the events of last night."

Jillian winced at that. "Does Bonnie have a lot of family?"

"She has an ex-husband," Hunter said. "And two grown children. The ex-husband is local, but her son lives in South Carolina and her daughter is in college in Florida. The kids are coming back to town, but the ex-husband wants to meet with me tonight."

"That sounds a little awkward," Jillian said. She thought of her ex-fiancé in California. She couldn't imagine having to deal with something as huge as a funeral for an ex. "They must have had a good relationship."

"I don't know. I hope so." He flashed her a teasing smile. "I've had enough drama for the day."

"I wonder if I ever met the man," Jillian said. "I assume his last name is Steck."

Hunter shook his head. "Vanderhook. Arthur Vanderhook. I think Steck was her maiden name. But you didn't answer my question. Dinner tomorrow?"

"I'd enjoy that."

Hunter stood, so Jillian rose with him. He gave her a kiss on the cheek before heading out. Jillian watched him go, though her mind was already on her next step. This ex-husband might know some interesting things about Bonnie, especially if they had stayed in touch. She headed into the kitchen.

Her grandmother was penciling notes on the remaining items on the order list. "Bertie," Jillian said. "Do you know anyone named Arthur Vanderhook?"

Bertie nodded. "Unfortunately. He was married to Bonnie Steck. I sometimes think people resort to divorce too casually, but leaving that man was the best decision Bonnie ever made."

"Oh? Was he abusive?"

"You mean did her hurt her physically?" Bertie shook her head. "Not as far as I know. But he found fault with everything she did. And he wasn't above spreading that bad temper around. I know he's been in bar fights more than once. Bonnie told me once that bailing him out of jail was the laundry's biggest expense."

"That sounds awful," Jillian said. "You don't happen to know where he lives?"

Bertie glanced at her sharply. "You're not planning to go over there, are you?"

"I might," Jillian said. "But I'm definitely going to finish my work first."

Bertie shook her head. "Absolutely not. Do not go over to that man's house. Promise me that. Just because he never hit Bonnie—as far as I know—doesn't mean he wouldn't hit you."

"Okay," Jillian said.

Her grandmother seemed content with Jillian's assurance and poked the next item on the order list—pumpkin pies. Jillian made a face. "You know I still haven't mastered piecrusts."

"I'll handle the crust and blind-bake them. You get going on the custard. Do enough for half a dozen pies."

Custard she could do, so Jillian walked back to the cooler for the eggs. As she did, her mind slipped back to the topic of Arthur Vanderhook. She still wanted to talk with Jasmine, but that conversation had slipped to a back burner compared to Bonnie's ex. Jillian was certain she needed to talk to the man, but she'd given her grandmother a promise, and she tried very hard not to go back on those. Luckily she knew exactly where Arthur Vanderhook was planning to be, and she knew she'd be safe there. All she had to do was crash a funeral consultation.

"I hope Hunter's in a forgiving mood," she whispered.

As she drove to the funeral home, Jillian was glad that she kept a change of clothes at the bakery for times when she needed to go somewhere unexpectedly. She felt badly enough about crashing the meeting without doing it covered in flour.

She pulled into the parking lot at Greyson & Sons and shut off the car. She sat in the car, gripping the steering wheel, waiting for either the courage to go in and risk messing up the best relationship she'd ever had, or the sense to go home instead. Finally she flung open the door and headed into the funeral home.

As always, there was an immediate hush when the door to the funeral home closed behind her. She wasn't sure if it was the thick plush carpet on the floor absorbing sound or just something about the somber atmosphere. The funeral home was certainly tastefully decorated and far from grim, with oil paintings on the walls and beautifully maintained antique furniture. Greyson & Sons had been in Moss Hollow for generations, and it showed.

Jillian walked down the hall, her shoes soundless on the thick carpet. Hunter didn't always meet with clients in his personal office, but she headed there anyway. There was the possibility that she'd arrived ahead of Arthur Vanderhook, and she could talk to Hunter about her plan before the man arrived.

When she reached the closed door, she raised her hand to knock and froze again. She wasn't afraid of Hunter, of course. Even if he was annoyed with her, he wouldn't react dangerously or even aggressively. It was just that their relationship was going so well, and Jillian was naturally superstitious about things that went too well. Surely it would eventually all blow up anyway. "Coward," she whispered, then rapped on the oak door.

She couldn't hear any sounds coming from the room, but that didn't really surprise her. The soundproofing all over the funeral home was impressive, which only added to the silence. It also gave clients privacy during the most vulnerable moments of their lives, the moments where they said goodbye to people they loved.

The door to the office opened and Hunter gave Jillian a surprised expression. "Jillian?" he said. "Is everything all right?"

She bobbed her head just once. "I'm sorry. Am I interrupting anything?"

Hunter's puzzled expression softened into a slight smile as he gestured for her to come in. "No, Mr. Vanderhook isn't due yet. But you're looking a little pale. Did something happen?"

Jillian stepped into the beautiful office with more of the fine antiques that characterized the whole building. "No, I just . . . I need to speak to Mr. Vanderhook, and I don't know his address or phone number, but I knew he was going to be here."

The smile slipped off Hunter's face. "So you thought you'd ambush one of my clients?"

"Not exactly." She knitted her fingers together, feeling as if she were already messing things up. "I heard this afternoon that there was bad blood between Mr. Vanderhook and Bonnie. He could be the one who killed her."

Hunter leaned against the edge of his desk, his gaze down as he brushed imaginary dust from its top. "You know I've always supported you, even though I have often wished you'd be more careful. I've sometimes stretched the boundaries of the acceptable to help you, but this is still a funeral home. People come here expecting professionalism and privacy."

"I know."

"Do you?" Hunter looked back up to lock eyes with Jillian.

"Because this doesn't exactly feel like it. You cannot talk to Mr. Vanderhook here. You simply cannot. And I'm more than a little disappointed that I need to spell that out."

"Of course," Jillian said softly. "I don't know what got into me. I'll be going."

Hunter glanced up at an antique clock on the carved mantel over the office's small fireplace. "That would be best. We'll talk later."

Jillian suspected she wouldn't enjoy the talk. It was obvious she'd pushed Hunter too far. She nodded and started for the office doorway, but it was suddenly blocked.

Hunter's assistant, Oliver Kent, peered at them owlishly through his large glasses, his smile so tense it was barely a slash across his thin face. "Mr. Greyson," Oliver said. "Mr. Vanderhook is here." Oliver stepped out of the doorway, and a big man stepped through it.

Arthur Vanderhook was about an inch shorter than Hunter, but he was so broad that Hunter, who was not a small man, seemed thin and scant in comparison. The man had a barrel-shaped chest and meaty hands, one of which he thrust out. Hunter took the man's hand and shook. From the way the knuckles of Vanderhook's hand whitened, Jillian could tell he was one of those men who turned a handshake into some kind of test of strength. To Hunter's credit, there was no visible change in his expression or body language as Vanderhook tried to grind his bones together.

"I'm so sorry for your loss," Hunter said quietly, his voice level and calm.

Vanderhook all but flung Hunter's hand away. "No big loss. Let's get this over with." He gave Jillian a once-over. "This your secretary?"

"No," Hunter said. "Miss Green was just leaving."

Since Hunter's manners were normally impeccable, Jillian knew his lack of introduction proved he was angry with her, no matter how calm his tone sounded. She smiled at him. "Thank you for your time." Then she nodded politely at Vanderhook and left the room.

"I'll walk you out," Oliver offered as he closed Hunter's office door.

Jillian barely noticed the man beside her as she struggled with a decision about what to do next. Hunter was mad at her, but she hoped that apologizing later would help him get over it. That didn't change her immediate need. She still needed to talk to Vanderhook, and she needed to do it somewhere outside of Greyson & Sons. That pretty much left her with a stakeout. She could follow Vanderhook when he left and speak with him wherever he ended up.

"Miss Green?"

Jillian's attention snapped back to the foyer of Greyson & Sons. Oliver was watching her with some concern. Obviously he'd spoken more than her name and she'd simply not heard him. "I'm sorry," she said with a smile. "I'm a little preoccupied. What did you say?"

He waved a hand. "Nothing, just a question about pastry. Please don't worry about it. I heard about your discovery of Ms. Steck. That must have been awful. I'm sorry that happened to you."

"Thank you," she said softly. "I'm sorry it happened to Bonnie. It must certainly be much harder on Mr. Vanderhook."

Oliver wrinkled his nose in a tiny moue of disapproval. "People respond to grief in many different ways. Not all of them are easy to be around."

"Of course." She reached out to pat Oliver's arm. "Thank you for walking me out."

Outside, the air was growing chillier as the darkness drained away any remaining warmth from the breeze. Jillian rubbed her arms, wishing she'd worn her jacket into the funeral home, but the air had been warmer then. She hurried across the parking lot to her car, studying the cars left in the lot. As there was no visitation scheduled, the cars in the lot were minimal. Jillian recognized Oliver's dark coupe near the end of the lot next to Mamie Cooper's light-colored sedan. Mamie handled makeup and hair for the funeral home; still, Jillian was surprised to see her come out of one of the doors near the back of the building and head toward her car.

"Mamie!" she called out.

The other women stopped and peered through the shadows left from the lampposts that stood at intervals around the lot. "Jillian?"

Jillian crossed the lot at a trot. "Yes, could you tell me something?"

Mamie shrugged. "Sure."

"I assume you'll be working on Bonnie's hair and makeup."

Mamie's expression became curious. "I will eventually. As coroner, Hunter has seen her, of course, but the body hasn't been released for funeral preparation yet. Maybe tomorrow. Why do you ask?"

"Well, I found the body," Jillian said. "I guess I feel some responsibility to her. Have you met any of her family?"

Mamie waved a hand toward the building. "Virtually everyone passes through here at one time or another. And I sometimes help with things like choosing the clothes for the deceased if people need it. You'd be surprised by how many people want to talk about things like that with someone, but I don't think most of Bonnie's family is in town yet."

"I talked to Hunter, but not terribly long," Jillian said. "Do you know if he found anything surprising when he examined Bonnie?"

Mamie shook her head. "Just that she had a bit of poison ivy on her forearm, which is common among gardeners in the South, so I assume Bonnie tended her own garden. That's about all I saw."

"Other than the head injury, do you know if there was sign of a prolonged struggle?"

"No. Nothing like that."

"Okay, thanks for talking to me."

"No problem." Mamie's gaze darted toward her car. "I need to get home before my cat decides I'm taking too long and destroys the place. He was feral before I got him and he can be a handful."

"It was kind of you to take him in."

Mamie laughed. "It's kind of him not to kill me in my sleep. I bet it's crossed his mind." She raised a hand. "I'll see you."

"Bye."

Jillian headed back to her car. She looked around for a possible hiding spot for her car. She was already in enough trouble with Hunter. She didn't want him to catch her holding a stakeout in his parking lot. Then she spotted a real estate sign in the yard across the street. She walked over and saw the house was completely empty. The driveway was partially shrouded by overhanging branches that would make it a great place to hide and watch for Vanderhook to leave.

Jillian's stomach growled loudly. She pulled out her phone and checked the time with a soft groan. *No wonder I'm starving.* Not only was she missing any chance at dinner with Bertie and Cornelia, her phone was nearly out of charge. *I really don't win a badge for being the most prepared tonight.*

She wondered if she had time to drive to the closest convenience store for a snack, but decided not to risk it. She just backed her car into the driveway and settled in, trying not to think about her grumbling stomach.

As it turned out, she would've had more than enough time to grab something to eat as she sat in the dark for at least an hour. She suspected she was about to start hallucinating cheeseburgers when her phone rang. Jillian fished it from her purse and saw the call was from Jasmine.

Jillian held her breath, hoping the phone didn't die during the call. Luckily, it was clear Jasmine wasn't interested in exchanging pleasantries as soon as Jillian answered. "I heard you found Bonnie Steck dead."

"Actually I found her injured," Jillian said. "She died later."

"Do you think that killer is the same one who burned my shop?" Jasmine demanded.

"I have no idea," Jillian admitted.

"But she was clutching one of those notes," Jasmine said. "The same notes we all got."

Jillian shifted in the car seat. Her legs were beginning to fall asleep. "Not the same. This note had nothing on the back."

"Has anyone else gotten two notes?"

"I don't know. We didn't get a second one at the bakery. Did you?"

"Not unless you count the note written on the whiteboard at Ayesha's station."

Jillian heard the tapping of Jasmine's long nails. "Have you got your bandages off?"

"I took them off," Jasmine snapped. "I couldn't do nothing with my hands wrapped up like that."

"Are you sure that's a good idea? Your burns could get infected."

"I'll worry about me, thank you," Jasmine said. "You figure out who burned my salon. And who killed Bonnie. 'Cause I think that's gonna be the same person."

"Maybe," Jillian agreed. Then she leaned sharply forward over the steering wheel. "I have to run, Jasmine, before my phone dies. I'll call you if I learn anything."

"You do that."

She saw Vanderhook stomp out of the funeral home and head for his car. His body language was a portrait of rage complete with tight fists at his sides. Jillian wondered if that was a steady state for the man or if something about the funeral preparations had angered him especially.

Hunter was normally really good at calming people, so Jillian was inclined to think this attitude had to come from something outside the meeting. She started her car as Vanderhook's low-slung convertible peeled out of the funeral home parking lot. She let him get a few houses down before pulling out of the driveway and falling in behind him.

Jillian suspected she was following closer than she should to be properly stealthy, but she worried about losing the dark-colored car if she let it get too far ahead. She gave a sigh of relief when Vanderhook pulled into the gravel lot of Cap's Place, a shabby hole-in-the-wall pub that served surprisingly tasty sandwiches.

As she parked, she realized she was actually going to have to go inside. She didn't make a habit of going to this particular pub alone, but Jillian could hardly strike up a casual conversation with Vanderhook otherwise. So she flung open her door and hopped out.

She'd been so busy talking herself into going inside, she hadn't noticed that Vanderhook was still in his car. As she walked toward the pub, the convertible's door flung open and Vanderhook heaved himself out of the car. "You!" the man bellowed. "Why are you following me?"

Jillian froze, then turned back to face him and pointed at herself. "You mean me?"

"Yeah, lady, I mean you. Like I wouldn't spot a white car following me on a dark night? Especially since Moss Hollow isn't exactly full of those little toy cars."

Jillian decided to pretend to be Bertie. She drew herself up as tall as possible and spoke with her grandmother's direct, annoyed tone. "My Prius is a perfectly grown-up car, but I have no idea what you're talking about. I assume we were heading here at the same time and you're having some kind of paranoid delusion about it."

Vanderhook narrowed his eyes at her. "You think I'm stupid or something?"

"I don't think much of anything about you at all," Jillian said loftily. "Except that you're standing in my way."

The big man gave a grunt of laughter. "Sure, someone like you is going to drink in Cap's all by yourself."

"Someone like me?" Jillian stuffed down a small spur of rising panic. Her Bertie impression did not seem to be winning the day. "I see no reason why you'd think you know anything about me. And I'm here for the food, not to drink."

Then, to her relief, she heard someone call her name. She looked around Vanderhook—no small feat since the man was so wide—and spotted Gooder Jones, dressed in jeans and a bomber jacket. Jillian smiled brightly at him and waved. "If you'll excuse me, I see my friend now."

Vanderhook spun and saw the deputy, who observed them with clear interest. Apparently the big man recognized Gooder because he shrank back away from Jillian. "My mistake," he growled.

"Clearly." Jillian swept by him, still trying for Bertie's imperious air, but her knees felt a little wobbly from relief. She walked the rest of the way across the parking lot, trying not to think about Vanderhook being somewhere behind her.

"Fancy seeing you here," Gooder said when she reached him.

Jillian linked her arm with his. "So, you gonna buy a girl some sweet tea?"

"Sweet tea?" Gooder asked with a laugh. "At Cap's you drink beer if you know what's good for you."

"Oh please," Jillian said. "You make it sound like a biker bar. It's not that bad."

"Bad enough." Gooder glanced past Jillian. "Was that Arthur Vanderhook you were talking to? I recommend you stay away from him. He plays rough."

"Then we better go inside before he gets here," Jillian whispered.

"He's not going to get here," Gooder said. "He just got in a car and took off."

Jillian spun back toward the parking lot. Sure enough, Vanderhook was gone. Jillian groaned. So much for asking him about his relationship with Bonnie.

Gooder pulled his arm from her grasp and put his hands on his hips. "Okay, Jillian, tell me what's going on. *Now.*"

"Sorry," Jillian said. "I would if I could, but I have no idea what's going on. Though I think somebody better figure it out soon before anyone else gets hurt."

12

Well, that could have gone better, Jillian thought as she stared glumly across the parking lot. Somehow, she was fairly certain a television sleuth would not have made such a spectacular mess of trying to tail someone.

She narrowed her eyes at Gooder. "Do you know where he lives?"

"Vanderhook? Maybe, but I'm not telling you." He smiled tightly. "Protect and serve, remember? It would not protect you to know his address so you can go poke the bear in his own den."

"Would it change your mind if I said I wouldn't go there alone?" she asked.

"No." Gooder took her by the arm and steered toward Cap's. "But I do think we need to sit down and chat."

He hauled her by one arm over to the bench outside the bar and plunked her down. Jillian wrapped her arms around herself. "It's too cold out here to chat. Honestly, it's been a long day and I want to go home."

Gooder shrugged out of his bomber jacket, revealing a flannel shirt underneath. He handed the jacket to Jillian. "I think this will stave off hypothermia long enough for you to tell me what you're up to."

Jillian would have loved to refuse the jacket in a display of toughness, but she was cold and the breeze was chilly. She shrugged into the jacket. It was warm and did cheer her up considerably. "I'm just trying to figure out who killed Bonnie. I know it's not the person who sent all the original notes." She held up her hand before Gooder could object. "If Pastor Keith says it's not, then I know it's not. So that means someone is trying to make it seem like the notes are tied to it, but what if they're not? What if it's just a murder committed by someone who hates Bonnie? I'm thinking her ex might fit that description."

Gooder sat down beside Jillian on the bench and stretched out his long legs, crossing them at the ankle. "I'm not saying that's a wild idea. Vanderhook is mean enough. He's been in trouble with the law more than once for bar fighting."

"I'm glad you see my point."

Gooder held up a hand. "But I don't think Vanderhook is smart enough for this kind of sneaky plan. The man is not exactly a poetry scholar. A head basher, yes. But the note? That just doesn't sound like something it would occur to him to do."

"Maybe he had help," Jillian suggested. "Maybe there's someone with a reason to protect him. Does he have a new wife or a girlfriend?"

"Not as far as I know. And we are looking into his possible involvement. We're looking into *anyone* with a grudge against Bonnie. Believe it or not, we do know how to do basic investigative work. We were solving crimes before the clever Jillian Green moved back to Moss Hollow."

Jillian didn't feel like fighting so she ignored the dig. "The last time I talked to you, you suspected Jasmine. I hope you've moved beyond that."

"As I recall, I said I had two good suspects: Jasmine and Bertie."

Jillian gave him a narrow-eyed glare. "Again, not funny."

"You say that you don't think your grandmother could kill someone. I could totally imagine Bertie taking someone out if they threatened her family."

"Which Bonnie didn't," Jillian snapped. "She just had some idiotic theories about the notes."

"She thought they were some kind of message for a specific set of sisters in Moss Hollow," Gooder said.

"But they weren't."

He shrugged. "So says you. I still haven't chatted with the note writer. Pastor Keith refuses to budge on revealing the identity, but why do I feel like you know more than you let on? And don't tell me the notes were some kind of weird message from the beyond sent to Cornelia."

Jillian stiffened. "Certainly not. Cornelia isn't into terrorizing the community."

"And the person Pastor Keith is shielding is?" Gooder asked.

"No," Jillian snapped.

"You know I could haul you in for obstruction," Gooder said. "If I harass the pastor, Sheriff Henderson will have me doing everyone's paperwork for a month, but he isn't nearly so fond of you."

Jillian closed her eyes and leaned back against the side of the building, not caring about the questionable cleanliness of such an action, especially since Gooder's jacket would pick up the worst of the dirt. *Which totally serves him right.* "I don't want to fight. Have you made any headway in finding out who set fire to Jasmine's salon?"

"It was an accident," Gooder said. "The fire marshal has ruled. A curling iron was left plugged in. It started the fire when it fell into a wastepaper basket. Unless you agree with the theory that Jasmine set the fire?"

"Hardly." Jillian opened one eye. "So you're not doing anything, even after I told you about the note on the whiteboard."

"I didn't say that," Gooder grumbled. "I said the fire marshal has ruled." He laced his fingers together and rested them on his stomach. "I checked on the whiteboard. I agree that it's suspicious, but it didn't lead to anything helpful. So, until I find more evidence, I can't do anything about the ruling. It stands for now."

"What about the note Bonnie was holding? Did you compare it to the others?"

"That's outside my skill set," Gooder admitted. "They all appeared the same to me, but I turned them in. There should be enough examples for some kind of determination. I should hear back about it tomorrow."

"In that case, it seems like there's nothing more for us to discuss." Jillian knew she should take off Gooder's jacket and head home, but she was suddenly exhausted at the thought. Right at the moment she was warm and relatively comfortable. Her stomach growled, reminding her that some things were still left undone.

Gooder laughed at the noise. "Someone's hungry."

Jillian pressed her hand to her stomach. "I have no idea how policemen survive stakeouts. I was starving."

"It helps to be prepared with snacks," Gooder said. He tapped on the wall behind them. "Shall we go in so you can get a sandwich? I wouldn't recommend this place for a lady alone, but I can sit with you while you eat."

"You don't think I can take care of myself?" Jillian asked.

"I would never be so foolish as to say that." He stood up and held out his hand. "Miss Green, want to have dinner with me?"

"I want dinner, but don't get any ideas about it being 'with you' or I'll tell my big scary mortician boyfriend," Jillian said. "And I agree with your assessment of Cap's, though I think the sandwiches are good."

"The sandwiches are fantastic. Sloppy and delicious."

He still held his hand out, so Jillian sighed and took it. Then, before Gooder could haul her to her feet, they were both distracted by the screech of brakes as a car seemed to practically leap into the parking lot and come to a stop nearby.

Jumping to her feet, Jillian gawked at the car, so distracted that she didn't let go of Gooder's hand. It was a big sedan with a long hood. Jillian didn't recognize the car, but she definitely recognized the little woman who flung open the car door and came hurtling toward them.

"You!" Ophelia Jones shrieked. "Get your filthy hands off my grandson!"

Jillian glanced down, squeaked, and yanked her hand away from Gooder's.

Gooder stepped in front of Jillian. "Now Nana Fee, this isn't what it looks like."

Ophelia Jones was shorter than Bertie Harper, but meaner. She wore her snow-white hair skinned back in a severe bun and nearly always wore a dress. She stormed toward them, leaving her car door hanging open. "I could not believe my ears when Corey Pace called me. She said my grandson was hanging around a bar with a loose woman. 'No,' I tell her. 'Not my Goodman.' I came right over and what do I find? Corey Pace was right."

"I am *not* a loose woman!" Jillian shouted as she came from behind Gooder.

Mrs. Jones poked her in the chest. "You have a man. Stay away from my grandson, Jezebel!"

"Nana, please," Gooder said.

Mrs. Jones grabbed Gooder by the sleeve. "You come with me. I cannot believe you are even here." She gave Jillian another sharp glare. "Is that the jacket I gave you for Christmas? Why is this floozy wearing your clothes?"

"She's not wearing my clothes," Gooder insisted. "She's borrowing my jacket. It's winter. She was cold, and I was being a gentleman."

Jillian was getting seriously annoyed at being talked about as if she weren't standing right there. She slipped out of the jacket and held it out. "And now I'm returning it."

"Good!" Mrs. Jones snatched the jacket from her hand, then pointed at her grandson. "Now get in the car, young man!"

"What if I have my own car?"

"Do you have your car?"

Gooder slumped slightly. "No, it's in the shop. That's why I came here. It's a short walk from my house. I don't need a ride."

"It is a short walk to drink beer and meet loose women. I should tell your mother."

"She doesn't care where I eat supper."

"And *that* is the problem!" Mrs. Jones yelled as she dragged Gooder toward the car. Jillian got the impression she'd be hauling him by his ear if she could reach it. "Mamas who do not care, who do not take proper care. That didn't happen in my day."

"I better go," Gooder told Jillian over his shoulder.

"Don't you talk to her," Mrs. Jones ordered, giving Jillian another death glare.

"Go somewhere else for dinner," Gooder called out.

Amusement and annoyance battled inside Jillian as she watched Ophelia Jones stuff her grandson into the car. It was nice to see someone take Gooder in hand once in a while, but Jillian really wished the woman would give up the idea that Jillian was after Gooder.

The big sedan roared out of the parking lot.

Jillian chuckled until her stomach chimed in with a rolling growl. Jillian looked back at the pub. They *did* have good sandwiches. It wasn't the sort of place she'd go alone after dark normally. But as she'd told Gooder, it wasn't some wild biker bar. She squared her shoulders and marched in.

Cap's was never exactly bright inside, but after dark it tended to be almost cave-like, with weak lamps and plenty of shadows pooling in the corners. A tiny, spindly Christmas tree sat on the end of the long bar, with a string of colored lights draped unevenly on it.

Bertie's theory was that the low light at Cap's hid questionable cleanliness. With her stomach growling like a cranky junkyard dog, Jillian didn't much care. She spotted an empty table in the corner and headed for it.

Cap's wasn't a big place and much of the room was taken up with a long bar, but it still managed to have a fairly impressive crowd for a weeknight. Jillian pored over the single-page sandwich menu, trying to decide between a Reuben and one of the house specialties. She finally settled on something called "the Stack" because it had lettuce, tomato, and avocado slices along with the ridiculous amount of meat and cheese. That way she could pretend she was having a well-balanced meal.

A lanky waiter obviously just out of his teens sauntered up to her table with a pad in his hand, and Jillian ordered the sandwich, then asked, "Do you have sweet tea?"

"Sometimes," the waiter said. "When Mrs. Cap comes by, but not tonight. We have soda."

She considered settling for water, but decided to go for a cola. Then before the waiter could take off, Jillian asked him, "Do you know Arthur Vanderhook?"

The young man rolled his eyes. "I should think. He's here enough. Though the next time he starts a fight, Cap is going to ban him for life." He gave her an appraising gaze. "You're not his girlfriend, are you?"

Jillian recoiled at the idea. *Must be my night for being accused of having weird taste in men.* "A million times no. Though I knew his ex."

"Ex? Oh, right—Bonnie at the laundry. I didn't know them when they were married. You think maybe it was being married to him that made her so crabby or the other way around?"

"I couldn't guess," Jillian said. "So Vanderhook doesn't talk about his ex in here?"

The waiter shook his head. "Naw, he talks about sports a lot. He bets on games, but he isn't very good at picking winners."

Apparently neither was Bonnie, Jillian thought. Then she had one last thought. "Do you know if Cap got one of those notes? I didn't see him at the town council meeting."

The waiter laughed at that. "Cap thinks the town council is made up of idiots, so I don't think he'd ever go to a meeting. I don't know if he got a note. He never talked about it."

Jillian's stomach took that moment to growl big and loud. The waiter smiled and tapped his pen on the pad. "I better go put this in so you can have your supper."

"Thanks."

Once the waiter walked away, Jillian examined the crowd. As expected, the pub was noisy with people talking and laughing in groups around the room. Surprisingly, the men perched on stools at the bar were among the quieter patrons. They seemed focused on their beers and staring at a basketball game on the small television screen. Jillian squinted at the screen. She didn't recognize the team jerseys, but she really wasn't a huge sports fan. She suspected Hunter could have told her.

The thought of Hunter made her sad. She hated that he was mad at her, especially since she deserved his ire. His reputation in the community was essential to his business, and she should have been more sensitive to that. The more she thought of it, the gloomier she felt.

"Why are you sitting here looking like someone just shot your dog?"

Jillian followed the voice to see Laura Lee Zane and wondered if it was law enforcement night at the pub. Laura Lee still wore her deputy's uniform, and her hair was pulled up into its usual ponytail. "Is Cap's a deputy hangout?" she asked.

Laura Lee slipped into the chair across from Jillian. "Not as far as I know. Gooder called me and said to come check and find out if you were in here eating alone. He seemed worried someone might come along and corrupt you." She glance around the room. "This bunch doesn't strike me as all that corrupt."

"Some of the folks at the bar might be a little sketchy," Jillian said. "What can you tell me about Arthur Vanderhook?"

Laura Lee shook her head. "I know the name, but I don't know the guy. They don't usually call me for the bar fights. Not that I couldn't handle them, but the Moss Hollow Sheriff's Department is the last bastion of Old World chivalry."

"Somehow I don't think of Gooder and chivalry together all that often."

Laura Lee laughed. "Gooder might surprise you. He's not a bad guy. You two just make each other crazy."

The waiter set Jillian's soda in front of her and asked Laura Lee if she was ordering. She told him to bring her whatever he was bringing Jillian. He scratched on his tablet and hurried away.

"You're trusting." Jillian took a long sip of the soda, hoping it would give her stomach something to do besides growl.

"I figure you know good food," Laura Lee said.

"So, is there anything you can tell me about Poppy's collapse or Bonnie's death?"

Laura Lee rested her forearms on the table. "Cutting right to the chase tonight. As far as I know Poppy's condition isn't a sheriff's department matter. She has been sick, and her doctor told us that probably messed with her blood sugar enough to make her a little confused. Lying out in the cold didn't help her any."

Jillian nodded. She already knew all that. "No sign that she could have been in an altercation with anyone? Strange bruises, anything like that?"

Her friend shook her head, sending her ponytail swinging. "I don't think so. We really aren't involved in it. There's no open investigation. Natural causes."

"Well, Bonnie's death certainly wasn't natural," Jillian said.

"No, that was murder, though Sheriff Henderson thinks it might have been a robbery gone wrong. Bonnie had no money on her or in her cashbox."

Jillian raised her eyebrows. "In a coin laundry, would she really have had much cash?"

"You might be surprised," Laura Lee said. "She also took in laundry and washed it for people. Apparently she made as much doing that as she did with the coin laundry."

"Of course, that doesn't explain the note," Jillian said.

Laura Lee shrugged. "The sheriff thought it might be two different things. Maybe Bonnie was carrying the note when she was robbed. Or maybe she had even created the note. The paper was common, and she had her other note on her desk in the corner of the laundry."

"Did she have a copy of the poem 'Goblin Market'? Because Bonnie didn't seem likely to know it. When she got her first note, she definitely didn't recognize the source material. So if she was writing a note, she wasn't working from memory."

"Good point," Laura Lee said.

"And the note in Bonnie's hand isn't the only suspicious note I've seen since Sunday," Jillian said. "I found something on one of the whiteboards at the Clip & Curl. Some kind of threat, from the look of it."

Laura Lee's eyes lit up with curiosity. "Do you remember exactly what it said?"

"Most of it was blasted away by the firefighters." Jillian felt the buzz of her phone through the side of her purse resting in her lap. She rooted through the purse and pulled out the phone. "Just a sec, Laura Lee. Hi Aunt Cornelia. What can I do for you?"

"Come home," her aunt said, her voice unusually hoarse. "Someone tried to kill Possum."

With that, Jillian's phone went dead.

13

Jillian borrowed Laura Lee's phone and tried to call Cornelia back, but the call rolled to voice mail. As she stood up, the waiter trotted toward their table with both sandwiches. "Wrap those up," Laura Lee told him. "Do it really fast and you'll get a bigger tip."

"You don't need to come," Jillian said as the young man raced away, no doubt in search of a doggie bag. "You should stay and eat."

"No," Laura Lee said flatly. "In fact, I should drive you, and you can pick up your car later."

"Don't be silly," Jillian said as she tried to force a smile. She was pretty sure all she managed was a grimace. She wasn't nearly as close to Possum as Cornelia, and sometimes she despaired of ever getting to wear black again without a fine coating of pale cat hair, but she was still fond of Possum. More importantly, she knew Cornelia would be devastated by any harm to the cat. "I can drive."

Laura Lee gave her an appraising look. Jillian laced her fingers together to hide the faint tremble she felt in them. "Fine," the deputy said. "But I'm following you. If I see any sign that you're impaired, I *will* pull you over and you *will* ride with me for the rest of the way."

"You're getting bossy in your old age," Jillian said, trying for a light tone.

Laura Lee smiled in reply. "So says the woman with a few years on me."

Jillian couldn't argue with that, so she smiled back and walked around the table. "I can't wait any longer. I need to get home. Cornelia must be in a state, and I don't know if she and Bertie are even safe."

"That's the kind of talk that'll get you a ride in my car," Laura Lee said sternly. "I'll collect the food and pay. You can go on out, but do *not* leave without me."

Jillian gave a single curt nod and headed for the door. She waited in her car for Laura Lee, but it took nearly all the self-control she had. Every second cranked her worry up another notch. When Laura Lee finally climbed into her car, Jillian didn't wait any longer. She headed for the street, trusting that her friend would catch up.

On the drive back to Belle Haven, only the knowledge that Laura Lee probably *would* pull her over kept Jillian from pushing her little car to top speed all the way home. Instead she whispered prayers as she drove and was grateful that the few traffic lights she encountered were green.

When she got to the house, she didn't even pull in under the porte cochere, instead stopping the car directly in front. She hit the ground running and nearly flew up the front steps.

"Cornelia!" Jillian shouted as soon as she came through the door. "Bertie!"

Her grandmother's voice came back clearly. "Kitchen!"

Jillian heard Laura Lee rushing in behind her, but she didn't pause. She hurried through the house to the kitchen.

Someone had spread out a couple thick towels on the kitchen counter and Possum lay on the towels. Dr. Shane West, Possum's vet, peered into the cat's eyes, and Jillian could hear Possum purring loudly as she walked up. The relief that swept through her made her a little weak in the knees.

"Is Possum going to be all right?" she asked.

The vet smiled up at her. "He's going to be fine. I think hitting the window reduced the force of the rock, so it just stunned Possum. He shows no sign of brain injury or skull fracture." He patted Cornelia's arm. "We can take him to the clinic, if you want, and I can do an X-ray, just to be sure."

Cornelia nodded. "That would make me feel better. Jillian, would you get his carrier out of the laundry room?"

"Sure, but what happened? What rock?"

Bertie leaned on the counter near Possum. "Someone threw a rock through one of the living room windows."

"Possum was lying on the floor near my feet," Cornelia said. "I made him get off the sofa because he wouldn't leave my book alone." Tears filled her eyes. "He wouldn't have been hit if I'd let him stay next to me."

"No!" Laura Lee said as she stepped around Jillian to face Cornelia. "Don't do that. It's not your fault. The fault here lies with whoever did this. Do you have any idea why someone would throw a rock through your window? Have you had any trouble with your neighbors?"

Laura Lee's strong tone drew the vet's attention. Jillian saw him very clearly checking out the young deputy. She knew Dr. West was single, and he was certainly nice. Even through her distress, she felt the tiniest tug toward matchmaking, but quickly squashed it. *It's neither the time nor the place.* She turned her full attention back to her grandmother's response.

"Our neighbors aren't really the rock-throwing sort," Bertie said. "And there's enough land between properties here that we don't have much chance to get on one another's nerves."

Cornelia stroked Possum gently as the vet peered into his ears. She gave Jillian a pleading face. "The carrier?"

"Of course." Jillian's mind whirled as she headed for the laundry room. Why *would* someone throw a rock through their window? A murder, a broken window, arson. Was Moss Hollow having some kind of a crime wave? And how much of it was related to the notes? Then she thought of the anger on Vanderhook's face when he'd confronted her in the parking lot of Cap's. If he knew who she was, he'd certainly had enough time to drive to Belle

Haven and chuck a rock through the window. *But why?* Even if he believed she was tailing him, what would he gain from throwing a rock through a window at Belle Haven?

She grabbed the carrier from beside the dryer and walked back to the kitchen. The vet and Cornelia were still fussing over Possum, but Bertie and Laura Lee were missing. Her aunt saw Jillian looking around and anticipated her question. "Laura Lee wanted to see the rock," Cornelia said. "Bertie and I never looked at the horrible thing. We were focused on Possum."

Jillian handed the carrier to her aunt. "I'm going to check it out too." She reached out and ran a hand down Possum's back. "I'm glad you're going to be okay, big guy."

Possum purred in reply.

She headed to the living room where Laura Lee squatted with Bertie standing over her. The broken window let a cold breeze into the room, and glass crunched under her shoes. "Find anything?" Jillian asked.

"This rock was customized just for y'all," Laura Lee said. "Come see."

Jillian squatted beside her friend, careful of the bits of glass. The rock was about the size of a softball, though it was more of a squashed oval than a sphere. And Jillian could see someone had scrawled on the rough surface with a marker. "'Your fault,'" Jillian read aloud. "Exactly what are they blaming us for?"

"The notes maybe," Bertie suggested. "That was the consensus on Sunday."

"But Bonnie moved on to blame Jasmine," Jillian said.

"Maybe someone circled back," Laura Lee said. "Maybe they're blaming you again. I think I should compare this writing with whatever is left on the whiteboard at the Clip & Curl. If someone is going after people they believe are connected with the notes, we need to find them, fast."

"Do you think you can get some fingerprints from the rock?" Bertie asked. "No one has touched it."

Laura Lee shook her head. "Probably not. Rough surfaces like that aren't great for fingerprints, but maybe we'll catch a break. I'll take it to the station, but first, I want to take a gander outside. Certainly whoever threw it was in your yard."

Jillian shuddered at the thought of someone with malicious intent being that close to Bertie and Cornelia.

Laura Lee picked up the rock carefully with a gloved hand and deposited it in a bag, which she laid on the sofa. "I'll come back through and get the rock before I leave."

"I'll go stay with Cornelia," Bertie said. "This has been hard on her. You know how she feels about that cat."

Jillian nodded. Though Bertie and Jillian were very fond of Possum, they both knew the cat had played a big part in helping Cornelia through her grief after her husband's death. Jillian suspected that emotion had gotten tangled into her feelings for Possum, and possibly played a part in Cornelia's quirky idea that Uncle Raymond communicated to her through the cat.

As they walked outside together, Laura Lee said, "If you've got some cardboard and tape, you should cover the window. It may be December, but you'll still get bugs drawn in by the light."

"I'll take care of it when we're done out here," Jillian said. "You know, I wonder if Arthur Vanderhook might have been the rock thrower."

Laura Lee raised her eyebrows. "He's obnoxious, but I don't think he's the sort to write notes on rocks. I'd believe it was him if he'd thrown the rock at you directly or just snuck up behind you and smacked you on the head with it."

"Don't you have a cheerful imagination," Jillian grumbled.

"Just calling it as I see it."

Jillian thought a moment. "Maybe he mistook Aunt Cornelia for me."

Laura Lee laughed. "Your aunt is shorter, and that red lion's mane of yours is hard to mistake for a head of short blonde curls. No, I doubt the rock was thrown at anyone. I think it was strictly meant to be a warning."

Jillian wrapped her arms around herself against the chilly breeze. "People should be hanging lights and exchanging Christmas cards, not ganging up on their neighbors and throwing rocks through windows."

Laura Lee swung a flashlight beam over the ground. "You might consider staying out of this."

"Not likely," Jillian said grimly. "Someone messed with my family. Aunt Cornelia or Bertie could have been seriously injured. We're fortunate that Possum's going to be okay. I can't stay away from it now. I have to do whatever I can to put a stop to all this."

Her friend sighed. "I don't suppose it would make any difference if I promise to find whoever threw the rock?"

"I appreciate it. But no."

"How about if I pinky swear?" Laura Lee asked, giving Jillian a sideways glance.

"Not even then. Laura Lee, someone set fire to Jasmine's shop. Someone bashed Bonnie in the head. And now someone has thrown a rock through our window. This has to stop."

"Those things might not be related."

"And Aunt Cornelia might not really believe in ghosts. But I know she does. And I know these things are connected."

"Can't say I didn't try to keep you out of trouble when Gooder and Hunter ask," Laura Lee said.

"You don't need to keep me out of trouble."

Her friend laughed. "Someone does. So what's your next move on the sleuthing trail?"

"I want to know where Vanderhook was when his wife died."

Laura Lee stopped laughing and gave her a stern look. "You are not to ask him directly. I'll find out from Gooder where he was. I know he was questioned."

"He was? Gooder didn't say anything."

"This might come as a surprise, but Gooder doesn't believe in sharing information with you. But I'll find out and let you know. Promise you won't go to see Vanderhook on your own."

"I won't go—for now," Jillian agreed. "And I promise I won't go alone if I do need to talk with him."

"I guess that's the best I can hope for." She sighed and put her hands on her hips. "I don't think I'm going to find anything in the dark. I'll come back tomorrow. Can you keep folks off the lawn until I get a chance to examine it in better light?"

"Yes."

"Then I'm going to grab that rock and head for the station."

"Good idea," Jillian said. As they walked back toward the house, she had a thought. "Have you ever met Dr. West?"

Laura Lee glanced toward the house. "The vet? I know who he is, but I've never met him before tonight."

"I should introduce you," Jillian said.

"Why? I don't have any pets."

Jillian smiled at her. "You never know when you might get one."

"You're a little strange," Laura Lee said with a laugh. "I like you, but sometimes I wonder if you spend too much time with your aunt."

Jillian grinned ruefully. "Sometimes I wonder that myself."

As she stared out the window at the darkness that gave lie to the word "morning" in December, Jillian absently crumbled a pumpkin muffin.

"What did that muffin ever do to you?" her grandmother asked. Jillian stared at her blankly. Bertie indicated the pile of crumbs on her plate. "I think it's dead."

Jillian winced. "Don't say that word please."

"Sorry," Bertie said. "What's bothering you, aside from everything?"

Jillian picked up one of the muffin crumbs and popped it into her mouth. She thought for a moment as she chewed. "I'm glad Possum's X-rays eased Cornelia's mind."

Bertie took a long sip of her coffee. "And mine. I may grumble about that cat now and then, but I'd hate to be without him."

"I'm glad they're sleeping in," Jillian said. "Cornelia was up so late."

"She's probably waiting until we leave so she can stuff the cat with bacon, but at least she agreed to call someone out to fix the window. It's one less thing on my plate."

Jillian could feel her grandmother's sharp appraisal, and she ate a few more bits of muffin, hoping to avoid an interrogation. Her hopes went unanswered.

"Something is bothering you besides Possum."

"There's a lot to be bothered about. I've come upon more than my share of crime scenes in the past week. Jasmine was a wreck over Poppy and her salon as well. I'm not one hundred percent sure Jasmine didn't attack Bonnie. She had reason to blame her for the fire at the salon."

Bertie frowned at that. "Jasmine wouldn't try to kill someone over a fire, no matter where it was."

"Maybe it was an accident?" Jillian ventured. "Maybe she got into a heated argument and things got out of hand? What if she thought Bonnie played a part in the fire *and* Poppy's condition?"

"Have you talked to her about it?" Bertie asked.

"A little on the phone," Jillian said. "But I think I need to see her face-to-face. And Jasmine isn't the only suspect. I don't like Bonnie's ex-husband. He seems like the kind of man who would cheerfully hurt someone."

Bertie took a long sip of coffee, studying Jillian over the edge of the mug. "What else?"

Jillian shifted in her seat. "What else what?"

"What's bothering you that you haven't mentioned? What are you trying not to tell me?" Bertie sighed. "Are you planning on doing something stupid and dangerous?"

"No," Jillian insisted. She tried to hold her grandmother's gaze, but no one could stare down Bertie Harper. "Okay, fine. Hunter is mad at me, and I feel terrible about it."

Bertie sat up straight. "What did you do?"

"Why do you assume *I* did something?" Jillian asked. "Maybe he's the one in the wrong."

"Is he?"

Jillian sighed and flipped a muffin crumb to the edge of her plate. "No."

"What are you going to do about it?" Bertie asked.

"I'll go talk to him after work or at lunch." Jillian sighed again. "We were supposed to have dinner tonight, but I don't know if he'll want to.'"

Bertie stood up and began gathering plates. "Don't wait until lunch. You can't go now. You'll wake the poor man up, and that's never a way to settle a disagreement. Once we get the bakery open, you need to drive over to Greyson & Sons and make up. I doubt either one of you will be able to think straight until you do."

"I doubt Hunter is having trouble thinking straight," Jillian said glumly. "He's probably making a list of the ways his life would improve without me in it."

"Don't be ridiculous." Bertie snatched the plate from in front of her. "Go finish getting ready. We'll need to get all the breads started so you can go mend that fence. And take him some pastries when you go. Everything is improved by a good pastry."

Jillian appreciated her grandmother's belief that The Chocolate Shoppe's pastries could cure anything, but she doubted this would be so easy.

Since she intended to leave as soon as the bakery opened, Jillian parked in one of the empty spaces in front of the bakery that were normally left for customers. The streetlights were still on, though the sky was beginning to lighten in the east.

For a moment, she stood still, enjoying the stillness of the early morning before the rush of shoppers and cars. Most of the stores were dark and their windows full of shadows. She spotted movement from the alley beside the shop and a small head peeked out. A dog with wiry fur took a step out of the dark, his tail wagging slowly.

Jillian smiled and knelt. "Hi there, fella. What are you doing here?"

The little dog leapt forward, his tail wagging furiously now that she'd shown herself friendly. He danced around as she tried to catch a glimpse of the tags hanging from his bright-blue collar.

"Grab him, will ya?"

Jillian rested a hand on the little dog's back as Ike Puckett strode down the sidewalk toward her. "The little monster took off before I could get his leash on."

"I didn't know you had a dog," Jillian said.

Ike huffed as he bent over to snap the leash on the dog's collar. "I don't. Jean got the thing from the shelter. She's hoping Gerald will get attached to a normal pet."

Since Gerald's last pet had been a snake that got loose from the hardware store the family owned, located across the alley from the bakery, and had ended up in the walls of Lenora's apartment, Jillian also wouldn't mind seeing the teenager focus on normal pets. "Is it working?"

"Only if Jean's real goal was to drive me crazy," Ike said. "The dog wrecks the house while the kids are in school, so I have to take it to work and walk it all day. And Gerald keeps complaining that the dog is scaring his snake."

"Sounds like a case of the cure being worse than the disease." Jillian stood and the little dog danced around her ankles. "He is a cute little thing."

Ike harrumphed but he leaned down and scooped up the little dog. "He's a menace." As he scratched the little dog's ears, Jillian suspected Ike himself was growing attached.

She reached out and chucked the dog under the chin. "Ike, did you get one of those poetry notes?"

Ike nodded. "I didn't pay it much mind. I don't have much experience with poetry. Honestly, at first I thought it was Jean dropping hints. She thinks I could be more romantic. I didn't keep the first one."

"First one?" Jillian said, surprised. "You got more than one?"

"There was one on the door when I came into the store this morning. You'd think folks would have something better to do at Christmastime."

"May I see it?"

"Sure," he said. "It's at the store. I'm going to give it to Deputy Jones. He came around for them yesterday." He led her to the shop and unlocked the door. Jillian followed him in, and then he locked the door behind them.

"You're in early," she said.

"I have to work on the books." He crossed the room and snatched a piece of paper from beside the cash register and held it out to her.

Jillian unfolded the note and glanced at it front and back. Like the note Bonnie was found clutching, it had no back-side writing. The quote was written in the same block letters she remembered. She read aloud. "'The stars rise, the moon bends her arc. Each glowworm winks her spark. Let us get home before the night grows dark.'"

"Weird," Ike said. "The whole business is weird. I read in the paper that Pastor Keith said they are harmless, but you'd think he could get them to stop if he knows so much."

"I think they did stop," Jillian said quietly. She handed Ike back the note. "I think the second notes are from someone else."

"Great, so it's catching." He dropped the note on the counter and wiped his hand on his pants.

"I think you're safe," Jillian said wryly. "Thanks for letting me see it. I best get to the bakery before my grandmother comes looking for me." She reached out and patted the little dog's head. "Goodbye. Oh, what's his name?"

"Trouble," Ike said.

Like Moss Hollow needs more trouble.

Ike let her out through the front door, and Jillian hurried back to the bakery, pulling her keys from her purse as she walked. Before she could put the key in the lock, she saw a slip of paper shoved into the crack between the door and the jamb. She plucked it out and unfolded it. It was another one-sided note: *She gorged on bitterness without a name: Ah! fool, to choose such part of soul-consuming care!*

She opened the door and carried the note inside. Bertie stood behind the front counter making coffee. "Nice of you to join us."

Jillian held up the note. "Someone is sending more poetry."

"I don't even want to see it. Take it to Gooder later. We need to get going on our work."

Jillian shoved the note in her purse and headed around the counter. "Aye, aye, Cap'n."

There was a long list of orders for everything from cake to cookies to various types of rolls. Jillian stayed so busy getting all the bread dough going that she didn't have time to fret. Well, not much time anyway. She did find her mind drifting back to the awkward interaction with Hunter once or twice, but a glare from Bertie snapped her out of it every time. A Bertie Harper death glare could cut through most preoccupation.

Jillian actually thought she was doing well until Bertie stopped her in the middle of rolling the industrial-size mixing bowl of white bread dough over to a long counter. "Leave it. Lenora and I can cut the rolls. Go see Hunter. Your moping is dragging down the mood of the bakery."

"It is not," Jillian said.

"It is, darlin'," Lenora called from across the room. "Go see your man. Get things settled. If he's as mopey as you are, he's probably scaring poor Oliver half to death."

"Fine, I'll go."

"And don't forget to take him some pastry," Bertie told her. "I'll box them up. Come on." She led the way out to the front counter and opened a box.

"I can box up pastry," Jillian protested.

"I know," Bertie told her as she slid open the back of the pastry case. "But this way you can tell him they're from me. It will make it look less like you're trying to buy his forgiveness."

"But isn't that exactly why you're sending them?"

"Of course," Bertie said, "but plausible deniability is important."

"You'd make a great spy." Jillian poured herself a cup of coffee in a foam cup. She hadn't slept well and was already feeling the effects.

"Take Hunter coffee too."

"He has a perfectly nice coffee maker," Jillian said. "I've seen it. It's fancier than ours."

"Fancy isn't everything," Bertie said. She reached into the pocket of her apron and shoved a piece of paper at Jillian. It was a check made out to Food for Less.

"What's this for?"

"After you make up with Hunter, run by the grocery," Bertie ordered. "Sal Roberto is holding a box of overripe bananas for me. We sell a lot of banana bread this time of year."

Jillian shoved the check into her pocket. "No problem." She took the box of pastry from the counter. "Are you sure I shouldn't wait until Maggie shows up?"

"She'll be along any minute. You go on." Bertie pushed Jillian toward the door.

"I'll be back as soon as I can."

Bertie waved that off. "Take as long as you need. Make things right with Hunter. He's a good man. Don't mess it up."

So much for taking my side, Jillian thought. "I'll do what I can."

"You do that," Bertie said. "Now let the folks in and get going." She nodded to the front door where Stewie Franks was peering in. When he saw Jillian and Bertie both looking in his direction, he waved through the door.

Jillian waved back and walked across the room, tucking the pastry box under her arm as she let him in. He nodded at her and mumbled a greeting. The two older women behind him glared at Jillian. "You're late opening!" one said.

Jillian glanced back at the clock over the cash register. "By two minutes."

"Late is late."

"Yes ma'am." She slipped by them and nearly ran into Gordon Sprague. The retired teacher was certainly spending a lot of time at the bakery lately. Jillian nodded to him as she ducked around him, and he nodded back.

The drive to the funeral home was quick since the traffic still hadn't reached the bustle that it was sure to have in an hour or so. Every day seemed to bring more Christmas shoppers out on the street, reminding Jillian again that she hadn't found a Christmas present for Hunter. *I hope he'll even take one from me.*

She reached the funeral home parking lot at exactly the same moment that a dark-silver Lexus arrived to turn in from the other direction. Jillian recognized the Lexus immediately, as well as the man behind the wheel. She smiled tentatively at Hunter.

He nodded and gestured for Jillian to go ahead. She steered into the parking lot as her stomach churned with nerves, making her more than a little sorry for the coffee she'd had. She pulled into the first space and Hunter pulled in right beside her. Since that wasn't his usual spot, Jillian had a panicky thought. *Is he trying to keep me from coming into his workplace again? Am I going to be banned from Greyson & Sons?*

She pushed open her door slowly and climbed out, her heart pounding. *Is this it? Is Hunter going to break up with me?*

Hunter climbed out of the Lexus, and Jillian was consumed by worry and guilt. "I'm sorry!" she said at the same instant that Hunter said the exact same words.

Jillian blinked stunned. "You're sorry? You didn't do anything."

He walked around her car to stand close to her. "I was cross with you. I don't want to be cross with you."

"But I did a terrible thing," Jillian said. "I know how important your job is."

He smiled slowly. "I know you do. It's just that your need to find answers and get justice for people sometimes gets the best of you. I know that. Good intentions don't always lead to good choices, but that's part of who you are, and I *like* who you are."

Jillian laughed in nervous relief. "I was so worried. I thought I might have done something I couldn't undo. I know how important this business is to you and your family."

Hunter smiled at her and squeezed her hands. "Greyson & Sons is part of my family history, and it *is* important. But you're a big part of my life. And I was worried too." He leaned over and kissed her.

"Are we still on for tonight?" Jillian asked.

"Wild horses couldn't keep me away. I'll pick you up at Belle Haven at seven?"

"You don't have to drive all the way out," Jillian said. "I could meet you."

"Picking you up is more fun," he said. "I get to see your grandmother and aunt beaming."

"Oh," Jillian said, the smile slipping from her face. "Aunt Cornelia will probably appreciate the cheering up. Someone threw a rock through the living room window last night and hit Possum."

"A rock?" Hunter's grip on her hands tightened. "Is he all right? I know Cornelia loves that cat."

Jillian nodded. "Dr. West came out. He said nothing was broken and did X-rays. But it was a hard night for Aunt Cornelia and Bertie."

"I can just imagine. Do you know who did it?"

Jillian shook her head. "The rock had the words 'your fault' written on it with a marker, but I don't even know what they're blaming us for."

"I don't like this at all," Hunter said. "Please be careful."

"I will. I promise."

Hunter let go of her hands, but his reluctance was clear. "I'll see you this evening."

Jillian gave him a sunny smile. "I'm looking forward to it." She started to hop back in her car, but saw the bag of pastries that Bertie had insisted she bring. Plucking the bag from the seat she turned to hand it to Hunter. "This is from Bertie."

Hunter took the bag and peeked inside. "My favorite. Thanks."

Jillian slid into the car, but she didn't pull away until Hunter had gone into the funeral home. She felt so much lighter now that she wasn't worried that their relationship was in danger.

The traffic had picked up a bit since her first drive through town. Jillian went through the events of the previous days in her head as she waited at traffic lights and crosswalks. Celia's friend Sidney had started everything off by sending notes to all the businesses in town. Some people reacted badly, getting scared and wanting someone to blame. At the city council meeting and at church Bonnie had come across as the leader of the angry portion of the population. By the time Sunday rolled around, that group even included people who weren't shop owners. Then the Clip & Curl had burned, and Poppy had collapsed. After that, Sidney came clean about the notes, but Bonnie died, in what seemed to be a robbery, with a new note clutched in her hand. Bonnie's ex seemed to be a good suspect, as he had a reputation for violence. Now new notes were appearing, but these, Jillian was certain, were not written by Sidney.

"And then there's the rock through our window," Jillian muttered. Lots of things were happening, and the one thread running through them all was the notes, but what was really going on? How had a high school project meant to prove Moss Hollow was a community that supported and trusted one another gone so far astray?

Jillian was so deep in thought, she nearly drove right by the grocery, and the car behind her honked at her last-minute signal. "Sorry," she whispered.

Since the grocery had only been open for the last hour, the parking lot was mostly empty, and Jillian was able to park near the entrance. The building was brick with big windows, all sporting large vinyl clings of snowflakes, cheery Santas, and dancing elves.

Food for Less was tiny compared to the mega grocery where Jillian had shopped in California. It didn't carry some of the more unusual items, but the produce was good and often grown locally. The store was nearly as big a hub of Moss Hollow gossip as the Clip & Curl. Now with the salon closed, Jillian wondered if she should pop into the grocery more often to see what people were saying about the notes and the happenings around the town.

She headed for the produce section, glancing down the narrow aisles as she walked in case she might spot someone she knew. Since it was still early, the store was impeccably clean and all the displays were neat and orderly. As she rounded the corner into the produce aisle, she stopped to admire a particularly attractive bin of oranges, their peels almost glowing in the store lights.

But her attention snapped away from the produce when she heard a booming male voice.

"Stop! You're killing me!"

Jillian wove among the produce bins, heading toward the sound of the voice. She walked around a tall cardboard display unit of spices and spotted Angie Brennen, the head chef at the Southern Peach Inn. She stood with her hands on her hips and her feet planted firmly, clearly annoyed with the man she faced. Jillian recognized him as well since he was the one who she'd come to talk to. Sal Roberto, the produce manager, waved his hands around as he shouted at her. "Always you complain. More than anyone else. Picky, picky, picky. I cannot work this way."

"Our guests expect the freshest ingredients," Angie said. "And that is what we will give them. If you can't do it, I suppose I can drive over to Painter's Ridge."

"Again with the threats." Sal gripped his chest. "You wound me. You truly do. I am an old man. My heart cannot take this abuse."

Angie sighed. "I didn't come here for the drama. Honestly, if you know you don't have something that is fresh enough, just tell me so I can get it elsewhere. Don't send me inferior goods. That's all I ask."

"Inferior goods!" He clutched at his chest again. "You are killing me." He spotted Jillian walking toward them and reached out to her as if hoping she would throw him a lifeline. "Tell this person that your grandmother loves my produce."

"She's certainly looking forward to the bananas I'm supposed to pick up," Jillian said mildly.

"Of course, I will go and get them. Anything for a good client." He glared at Angie, then spun and stormed away.

"Sorry," Jillian said. "I didn't mean for him to stop waiting on you."

Angie dropped her arms and shrugged. "It doesn't matter. Honestly, I'd just shop a wholesaler, but my boss insists we support local business." She sighed. "I need to go by the bakery this morning and pick up some rolls."

"Those will be fresh," Jillian said. "I set up the dough myself this morning so I can vouch for that." Then she had a thought. "May I ask you something? Did you see Bonnie Steck at last Sunday's brunch?"

Angie nodded. "Did I ever!" She frowned. "Honestly, I don't want to speak ill of the dead, but she and Mellie tried to rope me into their witch hunt over those silly notes. As if I had time to sit down with them. It was Sunday brunch."

Jillian raised her eyebrows. "I was under the impression they weren't interested in having extra people join them. In fact, I was specifically told that no one else was invited."

"That's not what they said to me. Bonnie complained about fair-weather protestors who wouldn't even risk the wrath of husbands to come to brunch. I remember that because she said those women didn't even know what it meant to *have* a wrathful husband."

"Sounds like the voice of experience," Jillian said.

"That's what I thought," Angie agreed. "I knew Bonnie had an ex, but that's about it. Sounds like he must have been quite a guy."

"I've met him," Jillian said. "He definitely has a temper."

Angie leaned against a heavy table holding a shiny metal washtub full of brightly colored apples and a pile of free recipe cards for different apple desserts. "So did Bonnie. You'd have thought getting a note full of weird poetry was the worst thing in the world. She insisted it had to be just the beginning, and we had to do something before phase two."

"Phase two?"

Angie shrugged again. "That's what she said. She was sure the poetry was just phase one of something much worse. I thought it was ridiculous, and since Bonnie was getting a little loud, I hid out in the kitchen until the two of them left. Thankfully, they were quick eaters."

Sal came back with a cardboard box, muttering under his breath. He thrust the box at Jillian and the scent of very ripe bananas filled the air. "You take these to your grandmother before they fill the whole produce section with fruit flies."

"Hold on, I have a check for you."

Jillian tried to hand the box to him so she could get the check, but Sal stepped back and waved his arms at Angie. "Why are you leaning on my table? This is not a bench."

Angie stood up and took the box from Jillian. "I'll hold it."

"Thanks." Jillian pulled out the check and handed it to Sal. "I'll need a receipt."

The produce manager harrumphed. "Then you need a cashier. Do I look like a cashier?"

"You look like a grouch," Angie volunteered.

Jillian took the box back, using the movement to hide her smile at Angie's comment. "I just need a receipt."

"Fine. I will get a receipt." He stomped away, grumbling about women in general, and bossy women in particular.

Angie laughed. From the hunch of Sal's shoulders, he wasn't quite out of hearing yet when she did. "Bertie should have come for the bananas. Sal wouldn't have dared mess with her."

"That could be true," Jillian said. "I'd better follow him and get the receipt. There's plenty of work waiting for me at the bakery. Thanks for your help."

Sal had only half a dozen more complaints about the stress in his life and the woman who put it there before Jillian left Food for Less, bananas in hand and receipt in purse. She thought again about what Angie had said. Bonnie and Mellie tried to get her to join them, and Bonnie complained that no one else wanted to be there. But she was sure that's not what she'd heard earlier. Or not exactly. It did make her curious. Could it be that one or more of the angry group at the church skipped brunch because they had a different plan? Maybe a plan to pull up fairies in Poppy's yard and leave Jasmine a message as well?

She was opening her car trunk and trying to come up with a mental list of the people she'd seen in that angry group in church when her phone rang. She shoved the box in the trunk and pulled out her phone. It was Laura Lee.

"How's Possum this morning?" the young deputy asked as soon as Jillian answered the phone.

"He's fine." Jillian slammed the trunk shut. "Actually, I didn't see him this morning, but I know he got a good report from the vet. The X-rays showed no injuries."

"Great. Do you have a minute? I have some updates that would get me in huge trouble with Gooder if he knew I was telling you, so I thought I'd call and share them."

"You know, he'd be hurt by your lack of fear," Jillian said as she got back into her car. "But I'm glad for it. Tell me what you know."

"I know Vanderhook has no alibi for the night of Bonnie's murder. He claims he was home reading a book. Does he seem like a book guy to you?"

He seemed more like a murder guy to me, Jillian thought, but she wasn't sure if that was being completely fair. "I'm not sure about anything these days."

"Well, I know this: The report came back on the two sets of notes, and the ones prior to Bonnie's murder were all written by the same person," Laura Lee said. "And the notes sent after Bonnie's murder were also all written by the same person, but not the same person as the first set."

The wash of relief surprised Jillian, and she rested her head on her forearm on the steering wheel. She'd been certain Sidney wasn't still sending notes, but it was nice to have it confirmed. Mostly, though, she was relieved that the sheriff's department knew someone else was sending notes now.

"The original note writer didn't mean any harm," Jillian said.

"So you and Pastor Keith keep telling us," Laura Lee replied.

"This new note writer is definitely not working from the same motivation," Jillian said. "Not with Bonnie murdered and a rock through our window."

"We don't know that the rock is from the note writer."

"When will you know?"

"When we catch him?" Laura Lee said, an inflection of uncertainty in her voice. "Our handwriting expert said she couldn't make any kind of definitive judgment over the words scrawled on the rock."

"How about fingerprints?"

"Nope. The rock is being examined for trace evidence, but I don't expect much from it. We're likely to find out that it's just an ordinary Georgia rock."

When the call ended, Jillian contemplated what she wanted to do next, and one idea leapt out at her. She needed to talk to Jasmine. She didn't want to believe Jasmine could hurt Bonnie, and she certainly couldn't picture Jasmine starting the note foolishness back up when it might have contributed to her salon fire and maybe even the collapse of her sister. But she had to admit Jasmine had motive in the attack on Bonnie. The note on the whiteboard certainly seemed to point back to Bonnie's embracing of Jasmine and Poppy as the culprits behind the notes.

As she tried to decide whether to make a slight detour before heading back to the bakery, she noticed the scent of bananas filling the car. She definitely shouldn't drive around with them in the trunk. Even in winter, the sun beating down on the car could transform the ripe bananas into a horrifying goo that would leak through the box and make her car stink forever.

"Guess Jasmine will wait until lunchtime," Jillian muttered as she started the car and headed for the bakery. She parked in the rear lot and carried the box of bananas in through the back door.

"Is that you, Jillian?" Bertie yelled from the storeroom.

"It's me. You want the bananas in there?"

Bertie walked out of the storeroom, wiping her hands on her apron. "No, grab one of the big mixing bowls and peel them all into it." Before Jillian could respond, she added. "You sort things out with Hunter?"

"We're good," Jillian said. "And I'll be having dinner with him tonight, so I won't be home."

Bertie smiled. "Good. You don't want to mess that up." She glanced at Jillian's mane of curls. "Don't forget a hairnet."

I wish, Jillian thought gloomily as she set the box down long enough to stuff her hair into one of the hideous pink nets. She then hauled the box into the kitchen and set it on a table before rolling one of the big bowls close enough to toss bananas into.

From the other end of the long table where she was scooping cookie dough onto a pan, Lenora smiled over at her. "I heard you settled things with Hunter. I'm glad."

Jillian took the first banana from the box, wincing slightly at its squishiness. "Me too. I thought I'd blown it."

"I expect you'll blow it a bunch of times," Lenora said. "It's part of being in a relationship."

"I suppose." Jillian studied her old friend. Lenora had a round face that never seemed to change with the passing years. She was pretty much exactly as Jillian remembered her from her childhood, albeit with a lot more gray in her hair. But today she seemed tired, worn, and old. "Are you all right?"

Lenora seemed to study the cookie scoop in her hand. "Poppy still hasn't woken up. The doctor says if she doesn't come around soon, she's not going to."

"I'm so sorry, Lenora," Jillian said softly. "And I'm sorry I didn't know her."

"She's a good person—a little flaky, but I never held that against her. It drove Jasmine crazy sometimes though. She used to say that Poppy was older, but she'd never been a proper big sister because she never gave up believing in silly things like fairies and wishes."

"Jasmine's going to have a lot to work through, I imagine," Jillian said.

Lenora nodded. "It's always hard when something like this happens, even when the person's always been sickly. Poppy must have been in the hospital a dozen times when they were kids."

"Maybe that's why she liked believing in magic," Jillian said.

"Maybe."

They fell into a companionable silence. For a while, the only sounds in the kitchen were the muffled sound of conversation from the customer area and the disturbing squish of each banana Jillian dropped into the mixer bowl.

When she finished peeling the last of the fruit, Jillian peered into the brownish mess. "I may never eat another banana."

"Your grandmother would tell you not to be such a wimp," Lenora said as she scraped the last of the cookie dough from another mixer bowl.

"And yet you don't see her out here peeling overripe, mushy bananas." Jillian gathered up the peels and carried them over to the pail where they collected compostable bits to take home to Cornelia's compost bin. Then she walked to the counter not far from the doorway to the customer area. The recipe files were stored in open crates on a shelf under the counter. Jillian pulled out the quick-bread bin and rooted for the recipe.

"Stop telling me to quiet down!" A male voice bellowed from the customer area.

Jillian set the recipe bin down and walked out into the customer area. Arthur Vanderhook stood on the other side of the counter. He jabbed a finger at her. "You! How dare you sic the police on me!"

Gordon Sprague stood up from one of the tables. "Arthur, maybe you ought to calm down."

Vanderhook spun and glared at the elderly gentleman. "And maybe you ought to mind your own business, old man."

While Vanderhook's back was to them, Jillian gave Maggie a sideways glance. The younger woman disappeared into the kitchen. Jillian knew Maggie was going to fetch Bertie, but she hoped she was calling the sheriff's department at the same time.

Jillian certainly didn't want him injuring any of their customers, so she called his attention back to herself. "I don't know what you're talking about," she said calmly.

"I'm talking about the cops rousting me out of bed on my day off," the man bellowed. "They practically accused me of killing Bonnie."

"I can't see what that has to do with me," Jillian said, making an effort to keep her voice calm and even.

"You think I'm stupid? I saw you flounce off across the parking lot at Cap's to talk to that deputy, and the next thing I know the sheriff's department is knocking at my door, just full of questions."

"You're the ex-husband of a murdered woman," Jillian said. "Questions were inevitable. Now, I'd appreciate it if you'd either order something or get out of my family's bakery."

Vanderhook leaned across the counter, giving Jillian a narrow-eyed glare. "And who's going to make me?"

"That would be me."

Vanderhook spun so quickly he actually had to grab the counter to keep his balance. Gooder stood in the doorway of the bakery with his arms crossed over his chest.

"I have a right to come in here, just like anyone else," Vanderhook snarled, straightening.

"To buy pastries, sure," Gooder said. "To harass the staff, no. So what are you going to buy?"

Vanderhook stared at him for a moment, his face reddening even as the knuckles of his tightly fisted hands turned white. Finally he said, "Nothin.'" Then he crossed the room and shoved open the door.

As soon as he was gone, all the customers joined together in a round of applause cheering Gooder.

"Just for that," Jillian said, "why don't you let me get you a cup of coffee and a bear claw?"

Gooder grinned at her. "I never say no to a bear claw."

Maggie came back through the doorway and resumed waiting on customers as Jillian brought Gooder a cup of coffee and the pastry in a small waxed-paper bag. The deputy stood by the door, out of the way of the customer tables. "Vanderhook came off a little guilty to me," she said quietly as she handed over the goodies. Then she gestured toward one of the empty tables.

Gooder fished the bear claw out of the bag as he followed her to the table. "Hard to say. He's always been a hothead." He took a big bite of the pastry. "Yum. I should throw people out of your bakery more often."

"But you did question him," Jillian said, as they sat. She waited for Gooder to chew and swallow another bite before he answered.

"It's my job," Gooder said. "His alibi is rubbish, since the only one who can verify it is his son, based on a phone call. Vanderhook said he was at home when he talked to the kid on the phone. But he used his cell, so he could have been standing over Bonnie's body when he made the call for all we know."

"That would be cold," Jillian said.

"And methodical," Gooder said. "But I don't think Arthur is either of those things."

"So you don't think it was Bonnie's ex? Then who are your suspects?"

"I suspect a mugger," Gooder said. "But I'd like to know who sent the note she was holding."

"You know the note is by a different person, not the one who sent a note to all the business owners."

"Yeah. And it's also nice to know Laura Lee is keeping you informed," Gooder said wryly. He took a sip of his coffee. "They might have been written by a different hand, but they have the same MO. All the shops are getting them."

"I wonder why," Jillian said.

Gooder took another sip of coffee. "I don't know. Off the record, that is one investigation I wouldn't mind seeing you pursue. There's nothing illegal in the notes, but they're making people jumpy, especially after Bonnie. I'd like to see that stop."

"Before something else terrible happens," Jillian said.

Gooder gazed morosely at the partial bear claw in his hand. "Yeah, before then. And I'm not sure we have much time."

Jillian shivered at his tone. She hoped he was wrong.

But for some reason, she doubted it.

After a busy morning, Jillian was almost looking forward to sitting down with Jasmine, just to get some time away from the bakery, if nothing else. As she drove through the traffic on Main Street, she suddenly decided not to show up empty-handed.

She headed for Food for Less and lucked into a parking spot near the entrance, which Jillian took as a sign she was doing the right thing. *Have to take my good omens where I can*, she thought.

She wove through the produce area to reach the deli. For once, no one was waiting for an order. The display counter was decorated with a thin tinsel garland, draped carefully to avoid obscuring the contents of the case. A tiny, stuffed, fleece snowman was perched on the top corner of the case.

As Jillian looked over the salad offerings, a woman walked over. She had one of the paper hats that the deli workers wore perched on her head, probably to distract from the ugly hairnet underneath. Jillian was surprised when she recognized the woman under the hat. It was Bess Holland. "Bess," Jillian said, "I didn't know you worked here."

"Just part-time," the woman said. "I come in a couple days a week and work the lunch hour. Every little bit helps these days. My kids want to be in everything, and between sports and dance classes, the costs add up."

"I'm sure," Jillian said. She looked over the salads in the case in front of her. "I need a little picnic for two."

"Oh?" Bess said, her voice knowing. "You and the handsome Mr. Greyson having a picnic?"

Jillian laughed at the interest on the woman's face. "No.

Actually, I'm having lunch with Jasmine. I thought I'd bring food since I think she's having trouble cooking with her burned hands."

"Oh, that's nice of you. She has been through a lot." Bess looked over the salads. "Do you know what you'd like for the picnic?"

"Honestly, I don't know. What do you recommend?"

"The chicken salad is really good here," Bess said. "And my husband loves the potato salad. I like mine without mustard, personally."

"They both sound good," Jillian said. "And maybe some pasta salad? Give me small containers of several things so Jasmine has choices. And leftovers."

Bess bent to begin scooping chicken salad into a container. "I never did understand it," she said.

"Understand what?"

"The point of figuring out what the poem was supposed to mean." Bess put the full container on the scale and punched buttons. "Who cares what the notes meant? I just wanted them to stop."

"You're not a shop owner," Jillian said. "You didn't get a note, did you?"

Bess shook her head as she snapped a plastic lid on the container. "No, but I heard about the notes, and they creeped me out. I just wanted everything back to normal."

"That's something we can all agree on," Jillian said.

Bess bent to scoop the potato salad. "Sorry for coming by the bakery. I guess I got caught up."

"Just out of curiosity, how did y'all get together? You don't still have meetings about those notes, do you?"

Bess rolled her eyes as she put the container on the scale. "We never did have meetings. The only meeting was the one Bonnie and Mellie had at the inn, and the rest of us weren't invited, no matter what she says. I think Mellie left us out on purpose, if you want to know the truth. She liked being Bonnie's right hand after

Jasmine became a suspect." She sighed. "It all sounds so stupid when I think about it."

"Now that Bonnie is dead, it's become a little more than stupid."

Bess began scooping potato salad into a container. "Mellie was so upset about that. She's the one who called everyone and said we needed to come find out what you knew so we could help track down Bonnie's killer." She looked directly at Jillian. "Those are calls I'm not taking anymore. We should have left it to the police to begin with."

"I appreciate that," Jillian said.

"I hope you're not trying to intimidate Bess!"

Jillian followed the slightly shrill voice and almost groaned aloud at the sight of Mellie Flanigan, tapping her toe with her arms crossed. *Maybe she's the one trying to look intimidating.* "What are you talking about?"

"Don't pretend," Mellie ordered. "I know you're trying to shut us up so no one looks into your buddy Jasmine for Bonnie's murder. But I'm not going to let my best friend's killer go free, no matter what you do."

"Mellie," Bess said as she looked nervously around, "Jillian is just ordering some lunch. She's a *customer.*"

Mellie smirked at that. "That just means I got here before she got around to the real reason for tracking you down."

"I didn't track her down," Jillian insisted. "I didn't even know Bess works here. I came in to get some food. You know, Mellie, your paranoia is a little scary."

"What's scary is that Jasmine has already killed in retaliation for her imagined arson, and no one is doing anything about it," Mellie said. "Who knows where she'll stop?"

Since Jillian had her own concerns about Jasmine, she wasn't completely sure how to respond, but she couldn't believe Mellie's melodramatic attitude.

"Mellie," Bess pleaded, "please, I could get in a lot of trouble over you accosting customers."

"Customer, my foot." Mellie pointed at Jillian. "She's not really here for the deli."

"Actually, I am," Jillian assured her.

Bess's eyes went round, and she made a small squeaking sound just before a man walked up to them. "Is there a problem?" asked Wit Doyle, who owned Food for Less.

"N-no, sir," Bess stammered. "I was just filling an order for this customer." She set the last of the containers of salad on the counter and offered Jillian a big smile. "Will that be all?"

"Yes, thank you. It looks great," Jillian said. She smiled at Mellie. "Nice to see you, Mellie."

Mellie's cheeks reddened, but clearly she was smart enough not to make any further scene in the face of Bess's clear panic. Instead, she gave a terse nod and stomped off.

"How are you today, Jillian?" Wit asked. He had the look of a man who'd once been very handsome, but was slowly softening into a comfortable middle age. He had a high forehead and dark hair shot with gray at the temples. He was always warm and welcoming to the Belle Haven women, along with everyone else in Moss Hollow.

"Just fine, Wit. And let me say that Bess was just doing her job. Mellie seems to be on a rip."

"Bess does great work for us." Wit turned his smile on Bess, who blushed slightly at the compliments. "We're lucky to have her."

"Well, it was nice to see you." Jillian gathered her deli cartons. "But I should pay for this and go. My picnic awaits."

The store owner shook his head. "Please, the food is on me. I'm sorry you had to experience any unpleasantness here in the store. But before you go, I would like to ask a quick question."

Jillian set the containers back on the counter so she could

pull a thin fabric grocery bag from her purse. "Thank you. What would you like to know?"

"I heard you are still looking into the notes," he said. "The ones that seem to keep coming despite the pastor's assertion that it was all over."

"The sheriff's department believes the notes going around now are from a different person," she said.

"Do you have any theories as to who is sending them?" he asked. "I had considered them some kind of harmless prank, but the town seems to be getting more and more worried. This isn't the Christmas spirit Moss Hollow normally embraces."

"I wish I had more than a theory," Jillian said. "But I certainly agree that they're upsetting people."

"I heard Bonnie's attack might be connected to the notes," he said.

"She had gotten one of the new notes," Jillian said carefully. "But there's no way to know if the attack was connected. Evidence suggests robbery."

The man's face darkened. "What if the new notes are a smoke screen? Maybe they cover someone's attempt to case businesses for robbery? Could one of the rest of us be next?"

"Not a comforting thought," Jillian said quietly. "So I certainly hope not."

"Me too," he replied grimly.

"Thank you for bringing lunch," Jasmine said. "My hands are feeling better, but they're still sore. You might have been right about my taking off the bandages too early." She waved a hand half-covered with stick-on bandage strips toward the food. "This looks wonderful."

"I'd love to take the credit," Jillian said. "But I picked the salads up at Food for Less, and I didn't even have to pay for them. The owner donated them."

Jasmine took a sip from the iced tea Jillian had poured for her. She set the glass down carefully. "That was nice of him."

"We can definitely agree on that," Jillian said. "Have you had a visit from Gooder?"

Jasmine raised her eyebrows in surprise. "No. Does Gooder know something about Poppy? I didn't think they were going to bother looking into who trashed her fairies, even if it might have brought on her attack."

Jillian felt of pang of sympathy. "No, I'm sorry. I thought maybe Gooder had talked to you about Bonnie."

Jasmine frowned. "No, though I don't know what I could tell him. I haven't exactly been on top of my laundry since Poppy's been in the hospital, and I probably wouldn't have taken it to Bonnie's laundromat anyway."

"I know you thought Bonnie might have been involved with your fire," Jillian said tentatively.

"I did think that," Jasmine agreed. "And if I hadn't had Poppy to worry about, Bonnie and I would have had words. I don't want to speak ill of the dead, but I still think she had a hand in the fire at the Clip & Curl. If nothing else, she instigated it by jumping on that ridiculous notion your grandmother tossed out there. You'd think the whole bunch would have more loyalty. First, we're all on the same side, then, bang, Poppy and I are the enemy."

"That's the thing about paranoia," Jillian said. "Once it gets going, it's hard to direct."

"Still, I expected better," Jasmine said. "From Mellie, if not from Bonnie."

"Why Mellie?" Jillian asked.

"She worked for me for a while," Jasmine said. "Doing nails. I would have kept her on, but she didn't like the work." She shrugged. "Some folks don't know a good thing when they got it."

"That's true," Jillian said.

Jasmine waved her hand. "I've got bigger things to think about. I haven't hardly had a minute to start sorting out the insurance stuff for the salon, what with being at the hospital most of the time." Then she blinked a few times. "Not that I don't want to be at the hospital. But it's hard, you know? Seeing Poppy all hooked up to stuff."

"I'm sure it is," Jillian said softly. "Lenora told me a little about how she's doing."

"Poppy's doing the same as she was," Jasmine said. "That's all they tell me. She's doing the same. Except they all look at me all moon-eyed and keep saying, 'we hope she recovers.'"

"People don't know what to say."

Jasmine sighed. "I know. It's just hard." She looked at Jillian sharply. "I heard you had some trouble out at Belle Haven."

Jillian was surprised. Normally, the Clip & Curl was a hub of Moss Hollow gossip, but with it closed from the fire, Jillian wondered where Jasmine had gotten her information. Lenora?

"Luckily no one was hurt, just scared."

"That is lucky. All this makes you think about how fast things change. One day everything is fine, and the next, nothing is fine. And there's nothing you can do about it."

"You can keep on keepin' on," Jillian said.

Jasmine took another sip of her tea. When she set the glass on the table, she said, "I reckon that's all any of us can do. Just keep on."

Jillian drove back to the bakery thinking her day had been awfully busy considering she had nothing to show for it. The kitchen was a stark contrast to the pleasant December afternoon coolness. Between the steamy proof boxes and the oven, the big room felt a bit like a sauna.

Lenora stood at one of the stainless steel tables, working apple pie filling into dough to make apple fritters, but she paused as Jillian tied on an apron. "How's my cousin doing?"

"As well as can be expected," Jillian said as she picked up the order clipboard from one of the counters. She was surprised to see most of the orders were done. She looked up from the clipboard. "I can't imagine what she's going through with Poppy."

Lenora began separating the dough into individual fritters. "So, you still think she conked Bonnie on the head?"

"I never said I thought that."

"Girl, everything you think runs across your face like a theater marquee. We all know you thought my cousin might have bashed Bonnie."

"Might," Jillian stressed. "She certainly had motive. But, no, I don't really think she did it. If I had to guess, I'd think Bonnie's ex-husband did it, though the business of sending out new notes seems kind of subtle for him."

Lenora paused again and wiped her forehead with the back of her hand, leaving a white streak. "What would he get out of bashing Bonnie?"

"I don't know. Revenge, maybe? I don't think their marriage ended well." Jillian sighed. "But that's all speculation. So I think I'll concentrate on baking." Then she laughed. "Now that's something I wouldn't have said when I lived in California."

"That's just water under the bridge," Lenora said. She resumed dividing the puffy mound of dough into smaller balls.

Jillian gathered the ingredients for the next item on the day's list—turtle brownies. As she worked, she made an effort to push thoughts of the last few days out of her head. She was going to have dinner with Hunter in a few hours, and he deserved to have her full attention, so she decided to put the mystery aside for the rest of the evening.

Standing in the storeroom and scooping flour into a big mixing bowl, Jillian mentally went through her wardrobe, planning what she would wear. That's when she saw Celia slip into the storeroom and walk over to write down her arrival time on the time-chart clipboard always hanging on the storage room wall. "Celia," Jillian called out. "Could you come here a second?"

Celia carried the clipboard over with her, scribbling as she walked. "Gotta be quick. Maggie is waiting on me so she can dash. If I make her miss her afternoon shopping, she's going to bite my nose off."

"I wanted to know how Sidney is doing," Jillian said. "You know, since the paper printed the story."

"Which story?" Celia asked. "The one that said the notes were harmless, or the one that said they're still coming?" She shook her head. "You know those new notes have nothing to do with Sidney, right?"

"Of course," Jillian said. "So does the sheriff's office. The handwriting is different, and even I could tell the paper was different."

"Somebody else is keeping this all stirred up, and Sidney already felt bad enough. Now she's blaming herself for Miss Steck's death. And folks are still scared."

"I'm sorry to hear it's still upsetting her. It's not her fault."

"I told her that," Celia said. "But she won't listen. She's so wrecked about it. But once we find out who sent them, she'll feel better."

"You mean once the sheriff's department finds out who sent them," Jillian said.

Celia rolled her eyes. "Like the deputies have time to track down someone writing poetry on notes. Sidney and I are doing our own investigating. You aren't the only one who can do the detective thing."

"Celia, that's not a good idea," Jillian said. "In fact, it's a dangerous, bad idea. You two need to stay out of this. Let it go. It's not Sidney's fault."

"How many times have people told you to let something go?" Celia asked. "And how many times did you listen?"

Jillian didn't say anything, but the answer must have been on her face.

"That's what I thought," Celia said. "Now, you'll have to excuse me. I've got to get to work. And I aim to get the job done." Celia spun on her heel and stalked off, slinging the clipboard at the counter under the nail where it normally hung.

Jillian watched her go with a sinking feeling. Short of sitting on them, she didn't think she could keep the teenagers out of the mess going on in town. And that meant she needed to figure out who was sending the notes and who attacked Bonnie before they got hurt.

As Hunter pulled his Lexus into the parking lot of Crazy Fish Bar & Grille, Jillian laughed out loud at what the restaurant's owners had done with the brightly colored wooden fish that decorated the outside of the building. Each fish now wore a muffler and a jaunty Santa hat.

"It's nice to hear you laugh," Hunter said. "That's one thing about my business. I don't get to hear a lot of laughter during the workday."

"That must be hard," Jillian said.

"I'm proud of what we do," Hunter said. "We give people a place to come together to grieve and begin to heal after a loss. We give them ceremony, and there is comfort in that too. But I definitely don't hear much laughter."

As they walked across the parking lot to the restaurant, Hunter reached out and took Jillian's hand, which surprised her. They didn't walk hand in hand much, and she wondered if his day had been even harder than he'd implied. She had to admit, the hand-holding was nice—a warm spot in the chilly evening.

Inside Crazy Fish, the whimsical Christmas theme continued with all the staff wearing the same kind of jaunty Santa hats as the fish on the side of the building. The hostess who greeted them also wore a necklace of glowing Christmas lights.

"You're looking very festive tonight," Jillian said as the hostess led them to a corner booth. "I love the fish decoration outside."

The young woman giggled. "That was the boss's idea. They make everyone smile."

"It was a good choice," Hunter said.

Jillian's gaze swept over the crowd as they walked. She spotted quite a few faces she recognized, but she couldn't have put a name with all of them. Though she spent most of her bakery time in the kitchen, she had still come to recognize most of the faces of folks from Moss Hollow from seeing them at the bakery, at church, or at the variety of different events she'd attended since moving back to her childhood home.

One face she could associate with a name returned her gaze with one that was decidedly unfriendly. Mellie Flanigan. To Jillian's surprise, she recognized the older man seated across from Mellie. It was Gordon Sprague. Jillian didn't think Mellie and Gordon got along. Their interaction at the bakery hadn't been particularly amicable, but here they were having dinner together.

Jillian jumped slightly as Hunter squeezed her hand. She blinked at him.

"This is our table," he said, his eyes twinkling. "Shall we sit at it or eat standing up?"

"Sorry, I was distracted."

"And that never happens," Hunter teased as Jillian quickly slipped into the booth.

The hostess ran through the specials so quickly Jillian felt a bit dizzy when the young woman finished and trotted back to the hostess stand. She looked down at the menu, then at Hunter. "Did any of the specials sound good?"

Hunter chuckled. "I'm not even sure what they were. But you have to admire her breath control to get them all out so fast."

When Hunter focused his attention on the menu, Jillian looked back toward the table where she'd seen Mellie and Gordon. They were gone, and she saw a busboy clearing the table.

"What has your attention?" Hunter asked.

"I saw Mellie Flanigan having dinner with Gordon Sprague. I didn't know they liked one another enough to eat together."

"I don't think I know either one of them particularly well," Hunter said mildly.

"They're both regulars at the bakery. Well, Gordon is. Mellie mostly comes in to complain, I think. But Gordon's been at the bakery constantly." She frowned as she thought about that. *Why is Gordon there all the time lately?* Before, he would often pop by once or twice a week, but normally he didn't linger. She tried to remember when he'd become a fixture.

"I know that look," Hunter said. "You're evaluating that man as a suspect, aren't you? You know, he might simply like baked goods."

"He does," Jillian agreed. "Especially muffins, but he has been hanging out at the bakery for hours a day lately, and Gordon's not really a hanging-out sort of guy."

"Maybe he's just lonely," Hunter suggested. "The holidays can be a lonely time."

"Maybe."

Hunter closed his menu and looked at her. "How well do you know him?"

"Not very. I mean, I've known him forever. He was my high school math teacher, but I didn't really think of teachers as people back then. They were these old fossils who were forcing me to do boring stuff to graduate."

Hunter chuckled. "I always pictured you as an ace student."

"I probably should have been," Jillian said, "but I was a little too caught up in my social life. Don't get me wrong. My grades were never bad. I was too focused on going to college to let them slide. But if the choice was between another hour or two of studying and some shenanigans with Savannah and James, I was out the door before you could say 'lickety-split.'" Then she smiled at him. "What kind of high school student were you?"

"I was a jock," Hunter said. "Baseball and track. Though I also loved shop class. I enjoyed working with my hands. I think I might have been a builder if the family business hadn't been calling."

"Are you ever sorry for that?" Jillian asked.

"Not really. I believe what I do is important, but I suppose everyone thinks 'what if' once in a while."

Jillian nodded. "And you have the house out on Bender's Creek to renovate. How is that project going?"

"It's mostly not," Hunter said. "I've been too busy lately, and we've had some rain. Though I really knew I wouldn't get much time to work over the holidays. I enjoy it when I'm there. It feels good to bring life back to something so old and neglected."

At that moment Amber, a waitress they both knew, rushed breathlessly to their table. "I'm so sorry for your wait. It's really busy tonight."

"It's no problem," Jillian said. "By the way, I noticed Mellie Flanigan and Gordon Sprague were having dinner together. Do you know if they come in often?"

Amber looked at her in confusion. "I have no idea who that is. But everyone comes to Crazy Fish." She smiled brightly, flashing white teeth at them. "Our food is crazy good!"

After taking their orders, Amber hustled off through the crowd. Hunter reached across the table and took Jillian's hand. "May I ask a favor?"

"Of course."

"Can we spend the rest of the evening talking about things that have nothing to do with this case?"

Jillian felt a pang of guilt, remembering that she had told herself at the bakery that she would set the mystery aside while she was with Hunter. One look at Mellie and Gordon, and she'd jumped right back into the fray. "Of course. I can't think of anything I'd rather do." She gave him a warm smile and squeezed his hand. Now all she had to do was keep her promise.

Easy peasy.

She hoped.

18

Jillian luxuriated in the feel of the leather seat under her, feeling full and content and more than a little pleased with herself. She'd managed to keep her promise through dinner, and she'd seen the appreciation on Hunter's face.

She wriggled a little in catlike happiness. She loved her little Prius, but sometimes she thought she could come to enjoy a nice luxury car. After the last few days, she was going to absorb whatever relaxation she could.

"I wonder what's going on up there."

Jillian's eyes snapped open, and she sat up in the seat to see what Hunter was talking about. Flashing lights from two sheriff's department cars had acted like a beacon to the curious, and Jillian saw the parking spots along Main Street were filling up even though the stores had closed. A couple of deputies held back the rubberneckers with sawhorse barricades and lots of hand waving.

"I hope it isn't another fire." She looked sideways at Hunter and considered asking if they could stop, but she remembered her promise at supper. "I'm sure I'll find out what happened tomorrow. That's one sure thing about the bakery." She tried for a careless laugh, hoping it sounded more believable than it felt.

"You don't have to wait until tomorrow. I'm not that cruel." He eased the Lexus to a stop near the group of onlookers. "Hop out, and I'll go find a parking place. Try not to get into trouble before I get back."

"I always *try*."

Jillian shivered when the cold air hit her after the warmth of the car. The cropped blazer she wore was more cute than cozy. Still, she could handle a little cold if it meant finding out what was going on.

She joined the nearest group huddled near the barricades. As soon as she spotted a familiar face, she moved closer. "What's going on?"

Lisa Flint, the owner of Print Worthy, stood beside her. "A break-in," she said, her eyes wide. "At Pearls Before Wine."

Jillian gasped softly. The cute little shop was one of her favorites, stuffed as it was with an eclectic assortment of vintage items. She didn't know the owner terribly well, but what she knew of Doreen Lytle, she liked. "Is Doreen all right?"

"I think so," Lisa said. "I don't know. I haven't seen her, though someone said she's in there with one of the deputies." Lisa stuffed her hands into the pockets of her jeans and hunched her shoulders. "First the laundry and now Doreen's shop. I'm starting to get worried."

"Do you know if Doreen got another poetry note recently?" Jillian asked.

With her gaze back on the store, Lisa nodded. "She mentioned it to me this morning when I saw her at the bakery getting coffee." She turned to look at Jillian. "Do you think the notes are related to all the things that have happened?"

"I don't know," Jillian said. "Mr. Doyle from Food for Less thought they might be. The new notes are by someone different than the first ones."

Lisa raised her eyebrows. "How do you know that?"

"The sheriff's department analyzed them," Jillian said.

"You do have the most interesting sources of information."

Jillian jumped when she felt a hand on the middle of her back. She glanced over her shoulder to see Hunter looking at her in concern. "You're shivering," he said.

"It's unusually cold," Jillian said. "But at least I have the windbreak of all these people."

Lisa laughed at that. "That's how penguins stay warm, you know. Only they're always shifting places so the cold penguins on the outside of the group move to the middle where it's warmer."

"Maybe I should try that." Jillian slipped through the crowd, moving toward the blockade.

"Jillian," Hunter said from behind her, but she pressed on. She hoped to speak with Laura Lee or even Doreen. As she wriggled through the press of people, she found it was warmer, until she emerged near the barricade, where the full force of the cold breeze hit her.

"Miss Green," Deputy Tom Shaw said.

"Is Laura Lee here?" Jillian asked.

"Nope, sorry. Deputy Zane has the night off." The deputy jerked his head toward the shop. "If you're thinking of trying to sneak in, Deputy Jones is there."

Jillian's spike of hope crashed. Gooder was definitely not going to invite her to a crime scene.

As she watched the shop door, Gooder stepped out and looked across the crowd. He spotted her and waved her over. "Jillian, come here, please."

From his stunned expression, Jillian assumed Deputy Shaw was as surprised as she was. She gave him a sweet smile as she stepped around the barricade. "Excuse me."

He bobbed his head. "Yes, ma'am."

When Jillian reached Gooder, he waved her into the shop. The second she was out of sight of the crowd, he rounded on her. "Come and talk to Ms. Lytle. She gets hysterical every time she looks at me."

"Why me?" Jillian asked.

"Because Laura Lee isn't here, and because you're a woman, and because you already know as much about what's going on as any of us. Now just go do it, please. I can't get anything coherent out of her." He aimed her across the room.

Doreen was sitting in a straight-backed chair behind the counter, clutching a cup of water. She looked up at Jillian and Gooder, and then burst into tears. Gooder gave Jillian a nudge forward. She walked over and knelt by the sobbing woman. "Doreen," she said gently, "are you injured?"

Doreen didn't stop crying, but she did shake her head vigorously. "That's good," Jillian said. "Can you tell me what happened?"

"I'm such an idiot," Doreen said between hiccupping sobs.

Jillian realized a sympathetic tone was not going to work with the weeping woman, so she took on her grandmother's no-nonsense approach to crying and spoke sternly. "I'm sure you're not. Now, have a sip of water and then take a deep breath. Then tell me what happened."

Doreen hitched a few breaths, then followed Jillian's directions. Finally she sniffled and said, "I had to take out the trash. The store was closed. I'd flipped the sign, but I think I forgot to lock the front door." She stopped and her eyes filled with tears.

"Everyone forgets things," Jillian said firmly. "You closed the shop, and you took out the trash. Then what?"

"I was coming back inside and I tripped over a box in the back room. It's kind of a mess back there. Anyway, when I did that, I heard a noise out front. I thought maybe someone had come in, thinking we were open." She paused and sniffed again but managed to keep it together. "When I got out here, I saw a jewelry tray on the counter. Someone had gone behind the counter and opened the display where I keep the antique jewelry. It was all gone."

"Are those the most valuable items in the shop?" Jillian asked.

Doreen looked around. "Not really. None of the pieces were worth much really. It was all costume jewelry and none of it was rare. Some of my antique toys in the window are worth more. I'd never put them in the window except that we don't get full sun in the winter on this side of the street." She blinked a few times. "The jewelry was smaller and easier to carry."

Jillian could tell Doreen was beginning to ramble. "Lisa Flint told me you'd gotten a second poetry note?"

Doreen nodded. "This morning. You don't think the two things are connected, do you?"

"We don't know," Gooder said, risking Doreen's tears by stepping closer. "Probably not. Someone probably just took advantage of the open door."

Doreen's eyes filled again. "You think? I'm such a scatterbrain at Christmas."

"Everyone is," Jillian said firmly, heading off the waterworks. "Did you see the person at all? Maybe a glimpse through the window?"

Doreen shook her head. "I was so focused on what was taken." Then she scrubbed at the tears on her cheeks with the heel of her hand. "Do you think he'll be back? Maybe I shouldn't have said some of the things here are more valuable." Her eyes darted around the room. "I don't want to end up like Bonnie."

"I'm sure that's not going to happen," Jillian said.

"Really?" Doreen's eyes were full of hope.

"You're safe now." And Jillian hoped she wasn't lying.

At that, Gooder tugged Jillian out from behind the counter. "I think I can handle things now. You can go."

"That's it? I get pushed out now?" Jillian asked.

"Yes. I have work to do. I can call Tom over to escort you out if you want."

"Thanks. I can find my way." Jillian stomped back to the barricade where she saw Hunter waiting. The look of relief on his face as he spotted Jillian approaching made her feel guilty. *I'm a terrible girlfriend*, she thought gloomily.

Later, as Jillian stood in her bathroom and stared at her face in the mirror, she thought how privileged she was to be in a relationship with Hunter, the most patient person she knew. He'd not only forgiven her for vanishing on him, he actually told her that he was proud of her for helping out. "I don't deserve him," she told the weary woman in the mirror.

She opened a jar of moisturizer and began dabbing it on her face as she thought about the robbery. Of all the people she could connect in any way with the first robbery and the attack on Bonnie, only one person really seemed like he might steal things and hurt people with little or no guilt: Arthur Vanderhook. Though he certainly wasn't connected with the original notes or the insanity that followed, he could have heard about them from Bonnie and decided to use them for his own ends. She could picture that.

"Of course," she told her mirror image as she rubbed the moisturizer into her neck, "he had no reason to break into the Clip & Curl." No one could expect to find much to steal in a beauty salon. But what if that was unrelated? What if that had been Bonnie after all? And what if Bonnie told her ex about it and unintentionally inspired him?

"But why would she tell him?" she asked herself. As far as she knew, they weren't close. Of course, in a moment of stress, someone might turn to the oddest people. "Take tonight. Gooder actually asked me to join him at a crime scene."

The woman in the mirror didn't seem to have any answers, only tired eyes and a slightly slimy cast to her skin, so Jillian switched off the light and headed off to bed. She didn't sleep well, and the dreams that visited her left her on edge when the alarm blasted her awake in the morning.

"Is Savannah planning to come in today?" Jillian asked Bertie when she got to the breakfast table.

Bertie eyed her suspiciously. "No, not now that Maggie is well. Why do you ask?"

"I thought she and I might do something together tonight," Jillian said, pointedly gazing at her toast as she buttered it.

"And you don't want to tell me what you have in mind." Jillian opened her mouth to protest, but Bertie held up her hand. "It's all right. As long as you don't do whatever fool thing you have in mind alone. Savannah has a good head on her shoulders."

Since both Savannah and Laura Lee had supported some of her wilder plans in the past, Jillian wasn't sure her grandmother's evaluation was fair, but she'd accept it. After breakfast, she called Savannah and explained what she had in mind. "If Vanderhook is the one breaking into shops, I want to catch him in the act. Unfortunately, he knows my car. So would you like to do some surveillance with me?"

"I can't think of anything I'd like better," Savannah said cheerfully. "And James has parent teacher meetings tonight so I'm totally free. Do you want me to pick you up from work?"

"Yes, I'll catch a ride in with Bertie. See you then."

When they opened the bakery, they soon discovered that nearly everyone knew Gooder had invited Jillian into Pearls Before Wine after the break-in. And everyone wanted to know why. So Jillian spent most of the day hiding in the kitchen. She even ate in the kitchen after Lenora brought her a sandwich.

Finally checking the last item off the order list, Jillian had to admit she'd gotten a lot done, even if it was exhausting.

Apparently her grandmother agreed. "If we keep this up, we'll make it through the holidays without falling behind."

"If we keep this up, we'll collapse from exhaustion and not care if we fall behind," Jillian said as she began wiping down the stainless steel counters.

Bertie laughed. "A little hard work never killed anyone."

"You say that, but I'm pretty sure it's not true. And personally I don't want to risk it."

Maggie poked her head through the doorway. "I've closed up, but I let in one last person." She moved aside to let Savannah pass.

"Am I early?" Savannah asked. "I can wait."

"No, you girls go ahead," Bertie said. "Lenora and I will finish the cleaning and lock up."

Jillian didn't have to be told twice. She took off her hairnet and apron, kissed her grandmother on the cheek, and dashed out with Savannah. "We'll have to go to Cap's and see if he shows up," Jillian said as they walked to the car. "Apparently he's a regular. I don't know his home address."

Savannah grinned at her. "I do. I come prepared."

"How did you find out where he lives?" Jillian asked. "I tried looking online with my smartphone but I couldn't find the address."

Savannah winked at her. "I can't reveal all my secrets."

Jillian laughed. "So you do his taxes?"

"You're no fun." Savannah stuck out her tongue.

The drive to Vanderhook's house didn't take long, and Jillian was glad to see the man's car in the driveway. "We haven't missed him. Unless he has two cars. Then we could wait out here for nothing."

"I don't think so," Savannah said. "The lights are on, and I saw movement by one of the windows. Should we go look in the window?"

Jillian thought about that for a moment, but before she'd made up her mind, the front door opened and Vanderhook stepped out, easily recognizable in the spill of light from inside the house. A young man stood in the doorway, giving Vanderhook an unhappy shake of the head. The older man just patted him on the arm and headed for his car.

"I wonder who the young guy is," Savannah said. "I don't recognize him."

"I think that might be a first," Jillian said. "I thought you knew everyone. I suspect that's the son. Hunter said he and his sister were coming in for the funeral. What I wonder is what's taking Vanderhook away from his family in this time of mourning."

"Sounds like our cue to find out."

When Vanderhook pulled his car out on the road, Savannah waited a beat before she pulled out on the road.

"I hope we don't lose him," Jillian said anxiously.

"We won't," Savannah assured her. "We don't want a repeat of how you said your surveillance went."

Jillian folded her arms. "It's not a competition."

Savannah gave her a quick grin. "It could be."

Jillian had to admit, Savannah did a much better job of hanging back and trusting her ability to avoid losing Vanderhook, which became challenging once they left town and moved onto some dark back roads where their headlights would stand out.

"How do you even know we haven't lost him already?" Jillian asked, as they hadn't seen the car in a while.

"I know this road. There aren't many turnoffs and most of those are a little washed out right now. If a car goes down any of them, they have to splash though mud and water. I just look down each one for signs of recent passage."

"How come everyone is better at this stuff than I am?" Jillian asked.

"James likes police shows and mysteries," Savannah said. "We watch a lot of them. It's very educational."

Jillian chuckled. "You sound like Cornelia." Still, she began to wonder if she should make a little more time for TV.

Finally Savannah bounced in her seat. "There, look. He took that road. That's hardly a road at all, but it looks like it's seen a lot of use tonight. Maybe someone out here is having a Christmas party."

"If I were having a Christmas party, Vanderhook would not be invited."

They crept down the bumpy dirt track that seemed to have been built by going around all the trees instead of cutting any down. As a result, the road twisted and turned like a snake. It was only the glimpse of light through the trees that made them realize they were nearing their destination.

Savannah stopped the car. "If I go any further, no one is going to miss our arrival. I saw a spot a few yards back where I can pull off the road. Then we could walk the rest of the way."

Jillian looked at the light through the trees and shivered despite the warm car. Sure, they could walk in the dark to a secluded spot where a murderer might be. What possibly could go wrong with that plan?

A shabby mobile home sat in the middle of a hard, red-clay clearing packed with cars. Light streamed from every window in the trailer. A few piled-up cinder blocks served as steps up to a warped front door. Jillian and Savannah didn't go to the door. Instead they crept around the trailer, looking for a spot where they might peer through a window.

They found it at the back of the trailer where a jumble of prickly bushes hid a discarded wooden table with one leg broken off. The table canted at a steep angle, but it did give them something to step up on to see in the window.

"Do you think this thing will hold our combined weights?" Jillian asked as she stepped up on the rim of the table.

"Who knows?" Savannah whispered merrily. "Time to live dangerously."

"You know," Jillian said, "you've become disquietingly cheerful since you got engaged."

Savannah leaned close to the window. Jillian scrambled up to join her. Though their perch was precarious, it certainly gave them the perfect view. Inside the trailer a single small room was mostly bare except for a round, felt-topped poker table, presently surrounded by men clutching cards and smoking cigars. A pile of money lay in the middle of the table, and Jillian could see Arthur Vanderhook scowling at his cards.

Jillian felt disappointment drop into her stomach. They'd staked the man out in order to catch poker night? "This is nothing," she whispered. She felt for the edge of the table to step back off, but the whole thing shook and another leg snapped, sending them careening to the ground and the edge of the table crashing into the side of the trailer. The commotion was definitely something the men inside couldn't have missed.

Jillian and Savannah scrambled out of the prickly bushes. They'd just gotten free when the men from the poker game came around the end of the trailer. Jillian was horrified to see Vanderhook among them.

Clearly he recognized her as he roared, "You!"

Another of the men slapped Vanderhook on the back. "What's the matter? Your old lady following you?"

"Hardly," Vanderhook snarled. He stomped over to Jillian and Savannah. "What are you two doing here?"

Jillian decided to try the offensive, mostly because no other idea presented itself. "I thought you might have robbed Pearls Before Wine last night. Is that where you got your poker money?"

"I got my poker money working," Vanderhook growled.

"Then where were you last night? Reading, like you were when your wife was murdered?" Jillian asked.

One of the other men stepped forward. "Hey, Hook was here last night. I won twenty bucks off him. He wasn't robbin' nobody."

Vanderhook sighed. "This is where I was on the night Bonnie died too."

"Why didn't you tell the deputy that?" Jillian asked.

Vanderhook's shoulders slumped. "My boss thinks I have a gambling problem, just because a bookie showed up at the job and made a fuss once. Anyway, my boss said if he heard of me gambling anymore, I'd be fired. I can't afford to get fired, so I couldn't exactly announce where I was when Bonnie died." He glared at Jillian. "And you'd better not either. My business is my business."

Jillian looked over at the other men. "Is that right? Were you men out here on Monday night?"

"You gonna tell my wife?" one of the men asked.

"No."

"Then yeah, I was here," the man said. "And so was Hook."

"Happy?" Vanderhook demanded. "Now get out of here."

They got out, but Jillian was far from happy. Her one real suspect definitely hadn't killed Bonnie Steck. So who had?

The gloom of having no idea what to do next followed Jillian all the way to work the next day, but one look at Lenora's face helped lift her spirits. The tall African-American woman's face positively glowed with joy.

"Poppy woke up this morning," she told Jillian and Bertie as soon as they came through the bakery door. "Jasmine called me. Poppy woke up, and she even told Jasmine to stop fussing. She's very weak, but she's awake. The doctor says she'll have some recovery time ahead, but it's finally looking good."

"I'm so glad. What wonderful news." Jillian gave her old friend a hug. "Did Poppy say anything about what happened the day she was hurt?"

"No, and the doctors said she was too weak to talk to the police yet. That will have to wait."

"Of course," Jillian said. "It will all come out in due time."

Lenora blinked back tears of joy. "I've been praying so hard," she said. "But I have to admit, I was worried. I'm so happy."

The glow of the moment swept away Jillian's sense of failure, and the kitchen was remarkably cheery all morning and into the early afternoon. Then Maggie popped into the kitchen during a lull. "Lenora," she called, "is Celia not coming in today? I was planning on getting out of here."

"She ought to be here," Lenora said. "That child is normally real responsible. Did you try her cell?"

"I did. It rolled to voice mail." Maggie crossed her arms over her chest. "Someone is going to have to come out here. I need to get going."

"I can do it," Jillian wiped her hands on her apron. "I just finished." She followed Maggie to the front, sweeping off the hairnet as she passed through the doorway. One benefit of dealing with customers was that Bertie only required hair be worn up, but it didn't have to be covered with the pink hairnets. "I'm sure Celia will be along soon. Maybe she had to stay after school."

Gordon Sprague was sitting at a table near the counter. "She's not at school. I saw Celia a little while ago."

"You did?" Maggie looked relieved. "Was she on her way?"

"Not really," Gordon said. "She was with another girl, poking around Bonnie's coin laundry when I drove by there earlier."

"Earlier?" Jillian echoed. "Earlier when?"

Gordon shrugged. "Around lunchtime."

"Are you sure it was Celia?" Jillian asked. "She should have been in school at that time of day."

Gordon nodded. "It was her all right. I thought maybe they had a day off. Seems like the school is constantly getting extra days off now that I'm retired."

"Look at it this way," Maggie said. "Now every day is a day off for you."

"Maggie, could you stay here just a few more minutes?" Jillian asked. "I want to run over to the coin laundry to see if the girls are still there. Then I can maybe bring Celia back with me."

Maggie didn't look happy but she finally said, "Yeah, I can stay a little longer, but don't get drawn off on some adventure. I need to get home."

"No adventures," Jillian promised. "I'll just go over to the laundry and come back."

"I can show you where I saw them," Gordon suggested. "I'll even drive. My car is right out front. I got a great parking place."

For a moment, Jillian hesitated, thinking how odd it was that Gordon was around all the time lately. *Is it a good idea to get in the car with him?* She gave herself a mental smack in the head. Gordon was hardly going to kidnap her after letting everyone in the bakery know she was leaving with him. "Thanks," she said. "That would be great."

When they got to the laundry, Jillian noticed the crime scene tape was gone, though a tiny scrap fluttered from the front doorframe. Two orange-and-white striped sawhorses were pulled across the front door, one of which sported a *Closed* sign.

The sight of the sawhorse depressed her. She thought of the man silhouetted in Vanderhook's doorway, the one who was probably Bonnie's son. What a horrible thing, to come home at holiday time in order to bury your mother. Her relationship with her own mother wasn't exactly close, but the thought of losing her made Jillian ache.

"The girls were around back," Gordon said, pointing. He pulled into the lot and parked in a space at the corner of the building.

"Could you tell what they were doing?" Jillian asked.

He shook his head. "I didn't really watch them at all. I was driving by and I recognized Celia and wondered about school. That's about it."

Jillian wondered why she needed Gordon along since he clearly didn't know anything about the girls. They walked around the building to the back where the pavement was more broken and weeds grew up through the cracks. Jillian saw three small outbuildings lined up at the back of the pavement, but there was no sign of the girls. "What are those for?" she asked.

"Bonnie had them put in when she expanded about ten years ago," Gordon said. "She said she had no storage room inside anymore so she added these."

Jillian raised an eyebrow. "You're a fount of information."

He huffed. "Try being retired. You don't have much else to do besides listen to gossip."

"Which brings me to a question I've had," Jillian said. "Not that we don't love having you around, but why have you been at the bakery so much lately?"

To her surprise, the older man blushed furiously. "Can't a man just like coffee and conversation?"

"Not if it makes him blush. So spill it. What's up?"

He scuffed his feet for a moment and cleared his throat. "I was wondering." More feet scuffing. "Is Bertie seeing anyone?"

Jillian blinked at him. "My grandmother? You're interested in my grandmother? Romantically?"

Gordon frowned. "Your grandmother is a fine woman."

"Who's about ten years older than you."

"I'm disappointed in you, Miss Green," he said primly. "I'd never expect you to be an ageist."

She didn't know what to say to that. The conversation had slipped into the twilight zone for her, so she turned her attention to the outbuildings instead.

"Bonnie certainly invested heavily in chain and padlocks. She must not have wanted anyone to get into them." She lifted one of the chains and rattled it against the door. In response, she heard a dull banging inside.

She and Gordon exchanged wide-eyed looks. "Someone is inside. It might be the girls. Do you have a crowbar or tire iron in your car?"

He shook his head.

Of course not. She should have brought her car. Bertie insisted they all carry a tire iron, and that would probably have done the job of breaking the handle off the door. "I'll go around and see if there's another way in. Sometimes these things have windows. If not, we'll need to call for help."

Gordon pulled out his phone. "I don't have any bars."

"Let me check for a window." She walked around the side of the building, then the back. She saw a grate near the roofline, but no windows. As she walked through the narrow space that separated the building from the one beside it, she pulled out her phone. She didn't have any bars either.

"I'll stay here," she called out. "You go get help."

Gordon didn't answer, so Jillian squeezed through the gap. The gap was tight enough that it didn't offer much view of the pavement until she'd popped back out. As soon as she did, she cried out in shock. Gordon Sprague lay sprawled on the ground, his head bloody. Mellie Flanigan stood over him, a tire iron in her hand.

20

"What are you doing?" Jillian asked.

"Only what I have to," the other woman said.

"Are Celia and Sidney in the shed?" Jillian asked, keeping her voice low and calm. Judging from Mellie's darting eyes and heavy breathing, she was more than a little on edge.

Mellie's head jerked in a sharp nod. "They called me," she said, "after they found my bracelet in the planter near the front door. They called to announce that they knew I killed Bonnie, and they were going to find more proof and call the police. I couldn't ignore that."

"Are the girls all right?" Jillian held her breath as she waited for the answer, forcing herself not to look at the blood oozing from Gordon's head.

"For now." Mellie stared at the tire iron in her hand. "I didn't want any of this to happen. None of this was my fault."

"Of course not," Jillian said gently. "How did you end up hurting Bonnie?" She decided to avoid using the word *killing* as long as possible. There was no point putting ideas in the stressed-out woman's head.

"I didn't mean to hurt her," Mellie said, her voice high and desperate. "She'd gone crazy."

"Crazy how?" Jillian asked.

Mellie waved the tire iron. "It's so unfair. It was her idea in the first place."

"Of course it was," Jillian said as she took a slow step toward the alley between the sheds. There was no way Mellie could hit her in there. There was no room. And if she ran through the tight space, she might be able to get away. Mellie wasn't exactly athletic. "Everyone knows Bonnie was volatile."

"Right," Mellie agreed, her voice losing the slightest bit of shrillness. "Bonnie was sure that Bertie was right and the notes were about Jasmine and Poppy. She's the one who thought we needed to send our own message. Called it phase two."

Jillian stopped moving, completely confused. "By burning down the Clip & Curl?"

"No!" Mellie howled. "That was an accident. I was just going to leave the note on the whiteboard and make a scorch mark on all the cover-ups. Like a black mark on Jasmine's business, you know? It was supposed to be symbolic."

"That's why you plugged in the curling iron," Jillian said. "To make the marks."

Mellie's head bobbed. "I knew how easy it was for those irons to scorch, and I knew where Jasmine hid her spare key. It was supposed to be simple."

"Until Jasmine showed up," Jillian said, the picture finally becoming clear.

"What was she doing there?" Mellie yelled. "She *never* goes in on Sunday."

"In your hurry to get away, you knocked the curling iron into the wastebasket."

Mellie drooped. "It was an accident."

"And Poppy?"

"That was all Bonnie. She pulled up the fairies and was going to dump them at Poppy's back door. But Poppy came out and started yelling at her, then just collapsed. It scared Bonnie half to death. She was afraid people would think she attacked Poppy. So she just ran off."

"Without calling for help," Jillian said sternly. "Poppy could have died."

"She panicked," Mellie insisted. "You don't understand. Bonnie and I weren't trying to hurt anyone."

"Then how did Bonnie end up hurt?"

"She decided she needed to come clean. *We* needed to come clean. Well, all she did was pull up some fairies. She hadn't even touched Poppy. But I accidentally burned up a building. What would happen to me when Bonnie faced up to her little prank? I would have ended up in jail, maybe even prison. No, I was not going to let that happen. We argued, and I slapped her across the face as hard as I could. She fell and hit her head. There was so much blood." She waved the tire iron at Gordon. "Just like that."

"You seem to be getting over your squeamishness."

"Yeah, it's amazing what you can get over with practice." Mellie narrowed her eyes at Jillian. "Now you're going to drag Gordon into the shed with the girls. I'll come back tonight when I figure what to do with you all."

Jillian waved a hand at the shed door. "How did you get the shed unlocked?"

"I didn't. Don't be stupid. I used bolt cutters to cut the lock and put on a new one."

"You have bolt cutters?" Jillian asked. "Who just *has* bolt cutters?"

Mellie shrugged. "They belonged to my dad. My garage is full of his old tools. My inheritance. So I brought them with me to gather up the girls. I knew these old sheds would be a great place to put them until I figured out what to do. And it was great until you showed up. Now you've stalled enough. It's time to get Gordon inside."

"Wait!" Jillian urged Mellie, hoping to keep her talking. "Who wrote the second round of notes? You? Bonnie?"

"I wrote them, but it was Bonnie's idea. I left one in her hand to try and throw the police off the trail. I threw the rock through your window too. I thought the 'your fault' message scratched on it would get the deputies thinking one of you Belle Haven women might be involved."

Jillian had stalled Mellie long enough. Her slow movements toward the shed put Gordon's body directly between her and Mellie. She hoped that would help slow Mellie down. She spun and sprinted for the gap between the sheds.

Mellie shouted from behind her. Jillian heard the sound of the tire iron clattering to the ground. She guessed Mellie must have tried to jump over Gordon and not made it. Jillian slowed to look and saw Gordon struggling weakly to hold onto Mellie, who was straining to reach the tire iron.

Jillian reversed direction and ran back, snatching up the tire iron just as Gordon collapsed again. Jillian pointed the iron at Mellie. "Hold it right there. I don't want to have to hit you, but I will."

"I don't think that will be necessary."

Jillian looked toward the laundry. Gooder ran their way with a gun in his hand. He looked at Gordon, then at the tire iron in Jillian's hand. "I hope you didn't do that."

"No, actually Gordon is the hero here." Jillian knelt next to the again-unconscious man and pressed her finger to his neck. She was relieved to feel a strong pulse. "He needs an ambulance. Mellie attacked him. She also burned the beauty salon, assaulted Bonnie, and I assume she sent the new notes and robbed Pearls Before Wine just to sow more chaos."

"I did *not* rob Pearls Before Wine!" Mellie shrieked. "That wasn't me!"

"It really wasn't," Gooder said mildly as he grabbed Mellie's arm and snapped on a handcuff. "We caught that guy. It was what we originally thought—just someone taking advantage of Doreen's moment of distraction."

Jillian gently took Gordon's hand. "We still need an ambulance."

"It's on the way," Gooder said. "Your grandmother called

when you didn't get back to the bakery fast enough. She said you'd come over here looking for her other harebrained help, and she expected me to fetch you out of whatever trouble you'd found. She told me I'd best bring an ambulance along because it seemed like you were constantly running across folks who needed them."

Jillian nodded. That sounded like Bertie. "It's a good thing you followed her suggestion."

"I didn't have the nerve to cross her."

"Hello?" Celia's voice called from inside the shed. "Can someone let us out? Please?"

"Where's the key, Mellie?" Jillian asked.

"It's in my jacket," Mellie said. "You can get it. I was never going to hurt the girls. They're just kids. You tell them, Jillian. I wouldn't hurt kids."

Jillian pulled the key out of Mellie's pocket. "Sure."

When she opened the shed door, she found the girls still tied up. Celia's skin was scraped from rubbing her face against the rough wall to pull her gag loose.

"Ouch," Jillian said as she bent to untie the girl. "That must have hurt."

"I figured whatever she had in mind was going to hurt more," Celia said. "Besides, I just asked myself what you would do. And I did that."

Jillian had to admit, that made her pretty proud.

On Sunday morning, Pastor Keith looked out over the congregation. His mild brown eyes seemed to look into each person and more than one looked away, despite the lack of accusation in the clergyman's gaze.

He smiled gently. "Moss Hollow has had a difficult time in the last week or so. We've had losses. And we've had near misses. We've had heroes." He smiled at Gordon Sprague, who sported a jaunty bandage on his head. "And we've been made to look long and hard into the mirror of our community and see the kind of people we are."

Jillian heard a soft sound, a rustle of discomfort pass through the congregation like a breeze across a grassy field.

"Most of you now know the identity of the young lady who sent the original notes. But do you know the motivation behind them?" His smile grew sad. "She wanted to prove something. She wanted to prove that the people of Moss Hollow are good people. That we are a community of citizens who genuinely care for each other. She honestly believed that a small town like Moss Hollow would reject fear and embrace love when faced with something we could not understand."

Again the soft rustle. Jillian could identify it now. It was guilt. Guilt that made it hard to sit still, even in the face of rebuke spoken in the gentlest of voices.

"We didn't quite live up to such youthful optimism, but I believe the opportunity hasn't completely passed. Fear has left some scars on our community. There are still some hard feelings, but I think we can be bigger than that. I think we can pull on that love that comes from our faith and our community, and we can walk in it."

The rustling stopped and every eye was on Pastor Keith. Jillian could practically hear the eagerness for redemption in the expressions around her. The congregation wanted to be what they'd always thought they were. They wanted to be the kind of community the pastor was describing.

"After service today, I'm going to collect all the cleaning supplies I have at my house and a hammer and nails as well. And I'm going over to the Clip & Curl. I'm going to help our sister Jasmine overcome the damage done by our fear. Some things cannot be undone, but some can. And so I will be there today to help restore the salon." Again he offered them his smile. "And I'd love to see some of y'all there too. Come and be the brothers and sisters we are called to be." His smile became slightly teasing. "Or come and help because you'd like to get the salon open again in time to get your hair done for Christmas. Come for whatever reason, but come. Let our sister see our love. Let our sister see how much family she still has in Moss Hollow. How about it?"

The chorus of "Amen!" and applause brought the pastor's smile to a full-spread grin. And Jillian found herself grinning right along. Along with the rest of the congregation, she had no doubt Moss Hollow would come through this time, stronger and closer than ever.

Hunter took her hand and gave it a squeeze. He leaned close to her. "How about it?" he whispered. "You want to join me after church for Moss Hollow's version of a barn raising?"

"A salon raising?" She grinned back at him. "Absolutely!"

Simple Assault & Buttery

Book Fourteen Recipe

Buttery Chocolate Shortbread Cookies

1 cup flour
½ cup confectioners' sugar
¼ cup unsweetened cocoa
    powder
½ cup unsalted butter, cold and
    cut into pieces

½ teaspoon of vanilla
⅛ teaspoon salt
1 tablespoon milk

Instructions

1. Sift together flour, sugar, cocoa powder, and salt. Cut in butter until mixture resembles coarse crumbs. Add vanilla and drizzle in milk while stirring, just until mixture comes together (it may not take the whole tablespoon). Shape dough into ball. Wrap dough in cling film and chill for 30 minutes.

2. Preheat oven to 300 degrees.

3. Roll out dough to ¼-inch thick. Cut into 2-inch x 3-inch rectangles. Place on cookie sheets leaving 1½ inches between cookies. Bake 20 to 25 minutes.

4. Cool completely on wire racks.

Up to this point, we've been doing all the writing. Now it's *your* turn!

Tell us what you think about this book, the characters, the bad guy, or anything else you'd like to share with us about this series. We can't wait to hear from *you*!

Log on to give us your feedback at:
https://www.surveymonkey.com/r/ChocolateShoppe

Annie's® FICTION